GUESS WHAT? WE'RE MARRIED!

Susan Meier

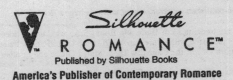

Silhouette
R O M A N C E™
Published by Silhouette Books
America's Publisher of Contemporary Romance

Thanks to Toby Keith
for performing the wonderful song
"We Were In Love."

 SILHOUETTE BOOKS

ISBN 0-373-19338-6

GUESS WHAT? WE'RE MARRIED!

***The first thing Grace saw when she
opened her eyes was an incredibly
handsome man sound asleep on the
chair beside her bed.***

Suddenly his eyes opened, and he and Grace
stared at each other.

Then wave after wave of feeling washed over her.

Somehow she knew they'd been intimate. As close
as two people could be. She knew there were deep
feelings between them. That they'd been through a
lot together…and that not all of it was happy.

But she loved him. Even without knowing who he
was, Grace knew she loved him.

She swallowed. "I don't know who you are."

"Then I guess I should tell you. I'm
Nick Spinelli.…"

And this time *he* swallowed. "Your husband."

* * * *

**Don't miss
THE RANCHER AND THE HEIRESS,**
the next book in the *Texas Family Ties*
miniseries, coming in June 1999,
only in Silhouette Romance.

Dear Reader,

Happy Holidays! Our gift to you is all the very best Romance has to offer, starting with *A Kiss, a Kid and a Mistletoe Bride* by RITA-Award winning author Lindsay Longford. In this VIRGIN BRIDES title, when a single dad returns home at Christmas, he encounters the golden girl he'd fallen for one magical night a lifetime ago. Can his kiss—and his kid—win her heart and make her a mistletoe mom?

Rising star Susan Meier continues her TEXAS FAMILY TIES miniseries with *Guess What? We're Married!* And no one is more shocked than the amnesiac bride in this sexy, surprising story! In *The Rich Gal's Rented Groom*, the next sparkling installment of Carolyn Zane's THE BRUBAKER BRIDES, a rugged ranch hand poses as Patsy Brubaker's husband at her ten-year high school reunion. But this gal voted Most Likely To Succeed won't rest till she wins her counterfeit hubby's heart! BUNDLES OF JOY meets BACHELOR GULCH in a fairy-tale romance by beloved author Sandra Steffen. When a shy beauty is about to accept *another* man's proposal, her true-blue *true* love returns to town, bearing *Burke's Christmas Surprise*.

Who wouldn't want to be *Stranded with a Tall, Dark Stranger*— especially an embittered ex-cop in need of a good woman's love? Laura Anthony's tale of transformation is perfect for the holidays! And speaking of transformations... Hayley Gardner weaves an adorable, uplifting tale of a Grinch-like hero who becomes a Santa Claus daddy when he receives *A Baby in His Stocking*.

And in the New Year, look for our fabulous new promotion FAMILY MATTERS and Romance's first-ever six-book continuity series, LOVING THE BOSS, in which office romance leads six friends down the aisle.

Happy Holidays!

Mary-Theresa Hussey
Senior Editor, Silhouette Romance

Please address questions and book requests to:
Silhouette Reader Service
U.S.: 3010 Walden Ave., P.O. Box 1325, Buffalo, NY 14269
Canadian: P.O. Box 609, Fort Erie, Ont. L2A 5X3

SUSAN MEIER

is the author of ten category romances. A full-time employee of a major defense contractor, Susan has also been a columnist for a small newspaper and a division manager of a charitable organization. But her greatest joy in life has always been her children, who constantly surprise and amaze her. Married for twenty years to her wonderful, understanding and gorgeous husband, Michael, Susan believes that being a mother, wife, sister and friend are life's real treasures. She not only cherishes those roles as gifts, she tries to convey the beauty and importance of loving relationships in her books.

OUR WEDDING VOWS:
TEN YEARS AGO

I, Grace Wright,

take you, Nick Spinelli,

to be my lawfully wedded husband.

I promise to be true to you

in good times and in bad,

in sickness and in health.

We shall love each other for all time

and be married forever....

Unless, of course, you skip town before the honeymoon.

Chapter One

Grace Wright stood at the foot of the spiral staircase and tried to look as if she was having a good time, though she was seething inside. Dressed in a slim and sophisticated pale blue bridesmaid's dress, which brought out the violet of her eyes and accented her thick, shoulder-length sable hair, Grace struggled to keep the smile on her face, but it was growing harder and harder.

Madison Delaney Kelly, Ryan Kelly's new bride, tossed her bouquet, and as if the stupid thing had eyes, it sailed unerringly in Grace's direction. When Grace moved to the right, Madison's younger sister attempted to grab the arrangement of roses and baby's breath and instead batted it into Grace's hands.

For a few seconds, everyone crowded around Grace, congratulating her and laughing about her good fortune, but Grace only smiled and nodded.

Fat chance that she'd be the next bride. The last thing she could do right now was get married.

Regret knotted into her anger as she realized her recent news was causing her to miss out of one of life's greatest pleasures, participating in the wedding of a sibling. Though Ryan Kelly wasn't really Grace's brother, he had been raised with Grace and her older brother Cal by rancher Angus MacFarland, and she thought of him as a brother. But her news had been so infuriating she couldn't stop thinking about it, and all she wanted to do was go home.

"Hey, Grace, looks like you're next," Ryan said, as he slid his arm around her shoulders affectionately.

Though Madison had opted for an ornate, extravagant gown, Ryan had chosen simple black tuxedos for himself and his groomsmen. But he didn't need anything more lavish. With his light brown hair and his sapphire blue eyes, he was attractive enough.

Because Grace didn't want to spoil Ryan's special day with *her* personal misery, she smiled and conceded the issue. "Yeah, looks like I'm next."

"Oh, don't pretend that upsets you," her older brother, Cal, said, walking up to them. Like Ryan he wore the simple black tuxedo. His usually tousled sandy brown hair was neat and orderly. His blue eyes danced with the delight of teasing his little sister. "You're ready to get married. I can see it in your eyes every time you look at a certain investment counselor." As he spoke, Cal glanced in Max Devereaux's direction and Grace fought the urge to weep. The perfect man had fallen into her hands as easily as the bouquet had moments ago, and she couldn't take advantage of it.

Ryan pushed back his cuff to peek at his watch. "Well, if you two will excuse me, I'm going to see if I can't find out what's taking the bride so long."

Grace rose to her tiptoes and kissed his cheek. "Have a good honeymoon and a wonderful life."

Ryan squeezed her hands. "I will."

When he was gone, Cal sighed heavily. "You two can be so obnoxiously mushy sometimes."

"Like you didn't cry at the ceremony," Grace said, linking her arm with her brother's as they strolled toward the open French doors which led to Madison's patio.

"I didn't."

"Yeah, right," she said, preceding her brother into the sunny garden.

"Well, at least I didn't look like I was going to spit on the bouquet when it landed in my hands."

Grace grimaced. "Was I that obvious?"

"Let's just say you confused old Beauregard over there."

"Stop calling him Beauregard. His name is Max."

"Max, Beauregard. What difference does it make?"

"It makes a heck of a difference. He knows you make fun of him."

"Yeah, but at least I didn't scowl when I caught a bouquet."

"You're just not going to let this drop, are you?"

"No, because I know you swoon over that refugee from Harvard's dean's list and I know you'd like nothing better than to date him and eventually marry him. It doesn't make any sense that you'd be upset over catching the bouquet, particularly since two true Ph.D.'s would see catching the bouquet as nothing more than a silly little superstition."

"It *is* nothing more than a silly little superstition."

"Then why are you wringing the stuffing out of those roses?"

Grace looked down and realized she had twisted the flowers to the point that she'd left a trail of petals. Shielding her eyes against the sun, she peered up at her brother and said, "Because I'm hoping to find my way out of the forest."

"No good. Madison has one hell of a garden here, but there's no way you can call it a forest. So, what gives?"

"Cal, can't you just let this be?"

"Nope."

She drew a long breath, saw that Max was safely tucked away at Angus's side—probably talking investments—and faced Cal again. "All right. I do like Max. I like him enough that I want to shift from a purely business relationship with him to one that's more personal, so I did something I hadn't thought about doing in the past ten years."

"Wow," Cal said, looking genuinely surprised. "He *must* be special. What did you do?"

"I tried to get a copy of my divorce papers."

Cal's face puckered with confusion. "Tried to get a copy of your *divorce papers?*"

"Well, I can only say I tried because I couldn't actually get a copy because there isn't a divorce decree to be copied."

"Grace, you're not married," Cal said carefully, his voice a hushed whisper.

She looked down at the bouquet she'd destroyed. "Yes, I am."

"What? How?" Cal said, grabbing her wrist and leading her deeper into the privacy of Madison's garden.

"Do you remember when Angus had his first heart attack?"

"Like it was yesterday. I had to figure out a way to get him to the hospital myself because I was the only one home. Ryan was out raising hell somewhere and you were staying overnight with a friend..."

Grace shook her head slowly to the right, then the left.

Openmouthed, Cal gaped at her, then, in spite of the fact that ten years had passed, Grace could see that clear memories dawned for Cal and he said, "The next day, Julie Kramer's parents didn't bring you home. You came home with..."

Grace pressed her palm across his mouth. "Don't say it. Don't even say his name. He left the day after we got married and I haven't seen him since. It wasn't easy, but I got over it, and now all I want is a divorce. Is that clear?''

Obviously hearing the sincerity and residual humiliation in her voice, Cal nodded.

"I can't believe it," Cal said when Grace removed her hand from his lips. "What are you going to do?"

"I hired a private investigator to track him down. He's come back to Texas."

"But not here?"

"Not even close. He lives in a teeny, tiny town called Turner."

"Have you called him?"

"No. I'm going to visit."

"Grace, I don't think that's such a good idea."

"I think it's a dandy idea," Grace said, ten years of pent-up frustration evident in her voice.

"Come on now, don't do something you're going to regret."

"Regret?" she asked, the word coming out in a gasp. "What I regret is marrying a man who deserted me when I needed him. I was sitting in a hospital worried to death that Angus wouldn't get through his bypass surgery, and Nick left a note in the mailbox telling me *he'd* decided we were too young to be married, but I didn't have to worry about anything because he'd take care of the divorce." She paused, drawing in a long, much-needed breath. "I wasn't too young. I knew exactly what we'd committed ourselves to when we took those vows, but apparently *he* didn't. And I never asked him to get the divorce. *He* volunteered. You would think he would have had the decency to do it."

"I know you'd like a little confrontation here," Cal said, trying to soothe her. "But this isn't the best way..."

"I don't want a confrontation and I don't want explanations. I want the divorce he promised me in that note, and I want it now," she said, glancing at Max and Angus again. "I could have one of Angus's lawyers handle this, but I think things will go more quickly, more smoothly, with both Nick and me available to sign papers and do whatever else needs done. That's why I'm going to Turner. It isn't because I want a confrontation. I want to make sure everything gets done when it needs to be done so I can get my divorce as quickly as possible."

"All right then, since you're determined to go, I'll come with you."

"You can't. I'm leaving tomorrow. And you and Angus have business in Houston tomorrow."

"Angus and I have business in Houston for the next two weeks," Cal corrected, sounding piqued. "If I didn't know better, I'd think you planned it that way."

Grace had the good manners to duck her head guiltily. "I did." She combed her fingers through her thick shoulder-length sable hair. "I never told Angus about the wedding."

"Obviously you didn't tell *anyone* about the wedding."

"So, you'll keep him busy in Houston and not let him send out a search party when he can't get ahold of me?"

Cal blew his breath out on a long sigh. "Yeah, I'll keep him busy."

"I mean it, Cal. I don't want him worrying. I swear, when I come back with the divorce decree in hand, I will explain everything. Until then, I need to keep him out of this, or he'll make it into a much bigger issue than it needs to be."

This time Cal glanced at her father. He smiled. "Don't you think it would be sort of fun to have Angus send a Texas Ranger after him or something?"

Grace gurgled with disgust. "If I thought he could keep it that simple, I wouldn't worry. But you and I both know Angus doesn't do anything by half-measures."

* * *

Sitting in a diner, finishing her cup of coffee, Grace drew a yellow line on the road map, linking her present location with the meager notation that represented the town of Turner. Satisfied that she would reach her destination before dark, she snapped the lid on her marker and slid it into her purse. She grabbed her wallet, fished out a few dollars, set them on the counter in front of her coffee cup, and put her wallet back in her purse. Map in hand, she checked the pocket of her pleated trousers for her keys, took one more glance to be sure her money was in front of her cup, then she walked out of the diner to her shiny red sports car.

Once her seatbelt was fastened, she drew a long breath and leaned her forehead against her steering wheel. *God, she was nervous.* When she was eighteen she'd loved Nick Spinelli with all her heart and she remembered him as being funny, rebellious and absolutely gorgeous. But the clearest memories she had of Nick were memories of their only night together, their wedding night. If she closed her eyes she could still see the firm muscle and sinew of his body. She could feel the press of his flesh against hers. She could hear the beat of his heart as she lay across his chest and fell asleep. She could smell him.

Deciding that particular train of thought wasn't wise, Grace straightened, pushed her key into the ignition, and pulled away from the diner. As she drove down the country road toward the highway, she wondered what their lives would be like if he hadn't left her. She knew she wouldn't have her degrees. She certainly wouldn't own her own business. She probably wouldn't be as close to Angus, Cal and Ryan.

And she probably wouldn't be lonely as hell.

She slapped the steering wheel. Who, or what, was to say her life with Nick would have been happy? The man had left her at their first sign of trouble. If Angus hadn't had a heart attack, they would have gone to California together. Undoubtedly they would have faced a hundred problems as a married couple, and given his reaction to the first challenge they faced, Grace knew he would have left her eventually. And she would be exactly where she was today. Nothing would be any different. She probably wouldn't be one iota happier.

Fighting the urge to close her eyes, Grace sighed heavily. She *wanted* to believe that. In fact, that logic kept her sane for the first year Nick was gone, when the pain was fresh and raw, when everything she saw reminded her of him and every holiday had her staring longingly at the door, praying he would come back for her. But now that she didn't need that logic for survival, now that she was older and wiser and knew the necessity of looking back on one's mistakes with a little objectivity, Grace had to admit Nick's leaving shouldn't have surprised her. She'd asked *him* to marry her. He hadn't asked her. He'd never once said he loved her. She thought he did, but he'd never actually said it.

A mature, intelligent twenty-eight-year-old woman could look back at the actions of an infatuated eighteen-year-old and admit the truth. Nick hadn't loved her. After ten years, Grace also wanted to believe she was mature enough to forgive him for leaving her, though that was still up in the air. But it almost didn't matter because they had bigger problems than their ten-year-old mistake. The truth was, she couldn't forgive him for not filing for divorce. She hadn't asked him to do that. He'd volunteered. Because he didn't get the divorce as he'd promised, not only was she forced to see him again, but he'd delayed her life… Again.

The pain of getting over him set her back nearly three years, and even after that, it had taken her another seven before she felt she could trust enough to love again. Now that she was finally ready to start over, she couldn't, because she was still married. And because she was still married, her conscience wouldn't even let her accept a *date* with Max. Which wasn't merely reason enough to be angry, it was reason enough to be strong, forceful and even downright single-minded in obtaining what she wanted and getting out quickly.

Satisfied with that rationale, she felt confident that she had enough perspective that she wouldn't make a fool of herself.

An hour later, Grace pulled off at another roadside diner. She needed a break, but she was also less than half an hour away from Nick's place. She didn't want to go to his house gritty and grumpy. She wanted to show him he hadn't ruined her life. She was strong, capable and independent. She wanted to gain his trust and cooperation so she could get her divorce easily. And she wanted to get the hell home. Period. End of story.

She turned off the engine of her car and reached for her purse, but couldn't find it. In fact, she searched her entire car and realized she'd been so preoccupied with her map, she must have left her purse at the last diner. Digging out some change from her car's ashtray, she found enough money for a soda and decided she could comb her fingers through her hair. She didn't want lipstick anyway. That way it wouldn't look like she'd fixed herself up for Nick.

After using the ladies' room and buying a take-out soda, Grace was in her car again. She glanced at the manila envelope on the seat beside her and thanked her lucky stars she hadn't put her marriage certificate in her purse as she'd intended. She could have someone wire money to her, but she couldn't substitute that certificate. Without that document, she probably couldn't get a divorce.

As she drove out of the gravel parking lot, Grace realized it was going to rain. Dark clouds billowed across the sky. The wind picked up. Sensing it was going to be one heck of a storm, Grace glanced at her map again. She had ten, maybe fifteen minutes of driving before she got to Turner. She knew the storm wouldn't hold off for that long, but because she didn't have money to buy a meal, she didn't want to wait it out in the diner, either.

Deciding to risk that this was nothing more than a good, solid autumn rain, Grace maneuvered her vehicle to the highway again.

The sky got darker and darker. Rain fell in sheets. Before she could make up her mind to pull off the road and wait for the worst to be over, a strong gust of wind blew her car to the right. The tires skidded into the gravel berm, and Grace overcompensated, throwing the vehicle into a spin. The last thing she remembered was that she was going to hit a tree.

Chapter Two

"**M**y what?"

Nick Spinelli fell to the arm of the leather sofa in the bedroom of his retreat in the Texas mountains, clutching the telephone receiver. Leftover wind from the recent storm blew in through the open French doors, cooling the room and bringing the clean, fresh scent of wet earth.

"I don't have a..." He almost said *wife,* but he stopped himself. If there was one thing Nick prized it was privacy. He wouldn't reveal a personal fact so quickly or so easily, not even when the answer came spontaneously because it was obvious. He *didn't* have a wife....

Actually, he did.

Praying there had been a mistake, he ran his hand down his face. "My wife's name is Grace," he said evenly to the woman on the phone, his tone not betraying the pounding of his heart. "You have my wife, *Grace Wright Spinelli?*"

The hospital representative confirmed the name and Nick collapsed against the sofa. *Grace.* He hadn't seen her in ten years, and now, not only was she a ten-minute drive away, but she'd been injured in a car accident. God only knew how badly.

"You have her at the hospital?" He paused, listening to the answer. "I'll be there in a few minutes."

Not bothering to change out of his jeans and sweatshirt, Nick forced his feet into old, worn tennis shoes and ran out to his Jimmy. In less than ten minutes he was at the rural hospital/medical center. The parking lot was very crowded, probably because of the short but severe storm. After Nick finally found a parking place, he pushed open his car door and bounded inside the hospital.

"I'm Nick Spinelli. Someone called me and said my wife was here," Nick told the smiling woman at the reception desk. She was tall, probably close to six feet, and her dark hair was peppered with gray.

She punched some keys on her computer and glanced up at him over the rim of her glasses. "Room 210."

"She's been admitted?" Nick asked, his worst fears seemingly confirmed.

The receptionist read from her computer screen again, then frowned. "I think you'd better talk with Dr. Ringer. He should be at the nurses' station on the second floor."

Blowing his breath out on a long sigh, Nick nodded and ran up the steps to the second floor. He didn't give himself a chance to think about what news might await him. He didn't give himself a chance to consider why his heart was pounding with fear. He simply ran.

As the receptionist had predicted, the doctor was waiting for him.

"I'm Nick Spinelli," he said, shaking the older man's hand. "You tended to my wife?"

"Yes, Mr. Spinelli. I'm Dr. Ringer," he said, motioning for Nick to follow him into a small room off the nurses' station. "Your wife was in an automobile accident. Along with a few bumps and bruises, she suffered a concussion."

Nick just barely stopped his sigh of relief. That didn't sound too bad. "So, she'll be okay?"

"Yes," Dr. Ringer said hesitantly. His blue eyes held Nick's for a minute, then he ran his fingers through his short gray hair. When he spoke again, it was carefully. "Physically she'll be fine in a few days, but her concussion has caused a memory loss. We're assuming it's temporary, but there's no way to tell how long 'temporary' will be."

For thirty seconds, Nick only stared at the doctor. Now that the initial shock of the situation had passed and he knew Grace was okay, he could think clearly again. News of her memory loss wasn't good, but it explained the fundamentals. Like why Grace didn't tell the authorities that though she was married to Nick, they hadn't seen each other in ten years. And why she hadn't asked to have someone else called—like Angus MacFarland or her brother Cal. And even why she hadn't protested that Nick himself had been contacted.

Unfortunately, her memory loss didn't answer some more important questions. Like how the authorities knew Nick was her husband, or even more curious, what the devil was she doing in Turner, Texas?

He was tempted to break his self-imposed rule of protection of privacy and ask some of the basics, but he bit his tongue. Because he was relatively new to the community and because he lived so far in the woods, no one would be surprised to discover they hadn't yet met his wife. However, in a town the size of Turner, if he mentioned that this woman was his wife but that they hadn't seen each other since the day after their wedding, more tongues would be wagging than tails at a dog show.

"Is there anything I should know before I see her?"

He was going to see her. He'd already prepared himself for that reality. To protect his privacy, he not only couldn't explain that they were separated, he also had to pretend to be a loving husband. But more than that, she was hurt and he was her husband. A strong, unexpected surge of instinct rose inside of him, compelling him to care for her when she couldn't care for herself. At the very least, he had to stay with her until Angus arrived.

"Well," Dr. Ringer said. "Obviously, you shouldn't say anything that will upset her. You also shouldn't force her to try to get her memory back. We've done the necessary testing and we're satisfied that there's no neurological damage, so she should regain her memory naturally. It might take a few days, maybe even a week or two, but her memory will be back. If you push her, though, you're going to upset her and that might delay the whole process."

"I understand," Nick said.

"You should also be aware that she's probably going to repeat herself, ask the same questions over and over. You'll need to bear with her. Do your best during the next few days not to get her riled up and everything will return to normal before you know it."

"Can I see her now?"

Dr. Ringer smiled. "You can see her now."

Grace was asleep when the two men entered her room. Her luxurious sable hair fanned across the pillow. Her eyes were closed, so Nick couldn't tell if they were the same beautiful violet color he remembered, but a light slanting in through the crack of the open door showed that her peaches-and-cream complexion hadn't lost its luster.

Swallowing back an emotion he didn't dare try to define, Nick whispered, "I thought people with concussions weren't supposed to sleep."

"Old medicine. Sleeping is fine. It's actually good for her."

Unable to stop himself, Nick reached for her hand. It was smooth and warm, just as he remembered. He stroked his fingers across her palm, up her wrist and to her forearm, feeling that he'd been granted an unexpected gift. He honestly never thought he'd see her again. Touching her felt like a miracle.

"Because her concussion resulted in memory loss, we'll need to keep her here under observation for a few days."

Nick nodded in agreement.

"If you have no other questions," Dr. Ringer said, "I'll be going."

Without looking away from Grace, Nick said, "No, I don't have any other questions. We're fine for now."

Smiling his understanding, the doctor turned to go, but changed his mind and faced Nick again. "You know, she didn't have any ID. No purse, no wallet. If it wasn't for the fact that your marriage certificate was sitting on the front seat of her car, we wouldn't have known to call you. I'm glad the paramedics found it."

Gazing at Grace, Nick nodded. "Yeah, me, too," he said, wondering why on earth she'd been driving around with their marriage certificate.

He waited until the doctor had left the room before he dragged a chair to her bedside. But he didn't sit right away. Instead, he studied the delicate features of Grace's face, her almond-shaped eyes, her pert little nose, her full lips and her dainty chin. The ten years that had passed had been very kind to her. She was even more beautiful than he remembered, and, he suspected, if he stayed long enough to be around when she opened those wonderful violet eyes, she would take his breath away.

Realizing it was a little too dangerous for him to be this close to temptation, Nick laid her arm across her stomach and moved away from the bed.

This was odd. Awkward. Yet unexpectedly wonderful. And he didn't know what the hell to do. He certainly didn't want to be around when she regained her memory.

They had a past that *couldn't* be straightened out. Yet he couldn't leave her either. He felt overjoyed to be granted the privilege of seeing her again...but he knew it was all wrong.

Walking back to her bed, he decided the right thing to do was to call Angus MacFarland. Since Dr. Ringer had explained that Grace had been found with no ID, Nick now knew Angus wouldn't have been informed of her accident, which was bad for two reasons. First, if Angus was expecting her home tonight, he'd be worried sick about her. Second, Angus should be seeing his adopted daughter through her recuperation, not Nick. Nick should be staying the hell away from her. He'd hurt her enough for one lifetime. And if he was smart, and Nick prided himself on being just that, he wouldn't hang around and risk hurting her again.

Using her bedside phone, Nick dialed directory assistance. He jotted down the number for Angus's ranch, disconnected and, not giving himself time to consider the consequences, immediately called the number. Though Nick wasn't too thrilled at the prospect of speaking to the temperamental old Scot who'd probably take him to task for deserting his daughter the day after he married her, Nick knew he didn't have a choice. Unless he wanted to explain to the hospital receptionist why he couldn't call his own father-in-law, he had to make this call personally.

The phone rang several times, and a man answered the phone. The stranger told Nick that he was the MacFarlands' housekeeper and that Mr. MacFarland had gone to Houston and wouldn't be back for two weeks. When Nick asked to speak with Cal, he was informed that Grace's older brother had also gone to Houston.

Without any further conversation, Nick hung up the phone. He'd felt uncomfortable about leaving a message for Angus. Something about the housekeeper's voice had sounded strange...maybe *temporary* was a better word for it. The man didn't seem trustworthy enough to deliver such an important message appropriately. Getting the news that Grace had been hurt in an automobile accident, without any explanation that she seemed okay, and without the reassurance of Nick's calm voice, might cause Angus to have another heart attack. In a way, Nick blamed himself for the first one. He didn't want to be a party to the second.

Confused, uncertain, he sat on the chair, then held Grace's hand again. Two weeks. It seemed like an eternity, but then again, it didn't seem like any time at all. Maybe staying with her wouldn't be so bad. After all, she didn't remember him, so she wouldn't remember what he'd done to her. He wasn't afraid of an ugly, angry scene, though that was a possibility he deserved. He was more afraid she would want an explanation. And he really didn't have one. At least not a good one. So, in a way, it was almost better if she didn't get her memory back until Angus and Cal returned.

In a way.

In another way, it was the worst thing that could happen. He didn't start his next assignment until the middle of November, which gave him six weeks. He could care for her for the two weeks Angus and Cal would be away, but the question was, did he want to? He'd made a clean break from her ten years ago. It wasn't nice and it wasn't easy, but he'd gotten them out of the worst mistake of their lives.

He glanced at Grace's luminous skin, the rich bounty of sable hair, her full lips, which, even in sleep, were bowed upward. No, it wasn't really wise to get involved again. His past was gone. His life was different. He didn't want to open up old wounds, particularly when they'd been neatly closed, very neatly closed, for the past five years.

The day after Nick and Grace were married, they returned to Crossroads Creek and discovered her adoptive father, Angus, had had a heart attack. Nick agreed to let Grace go to the hospital alone rather than complicate the situation. Instead he returned to his parents' home to pack for their trip to California in the morning. When he arrived, his father was drunk and screaming at his mother. From past experience, Nick knew that unless he diffused the situation, his father would soon go from screaming to hitting, and he stormed into the house.

In that second, as he ran to save his mother, another even more frightening, absolutely debilitating realization dawned on eighteen-year-old Nick.

All through high school, even while he dated Grace, Nick had managed to keep his life a secret from her. But by marrying her, he'd pulled her into his family...and his problems. Fear flooded him, because being part of this family was sometimes dangerous, but humiliation overrode the fear.

What would she think of him if she knew how he lived? What would she think if she learned he didn't work for spending money, but to pay the family bills? What would she think the first time she witnessed one of his father's drunken tirades and knew that same blood that flowed through Jake Spinelli's veins also flowed through Nick's?

It hadn't taken long for Nick to realize he couldn't put Grace in danger, any more than he could face the humiliation of having the woman he loved discover his family secret. Right then, Nick decided he couldn't subject Grace to this life. He wrote her a note, got on his bike, and left Crossroads Creek forever.

Though he'd loved Grace desperately, he managed to get beyond the pain.

His father died a week after he graduated from college and Nick set up his mother in an apartment near her own family in Dallas. He didn't go back to Crossroads Creek. He didn't think about his father, about high school, about scraping for money to support his mother... And seeing Grace only brought it all back again.

He glanced at the shiny brown lashes lying against her cheek. But how could he desert her now?

Nick sighed and leaned against the hard back of the old plastic chair. Never before had he felt so torn. Even when he'd left ten years ago, the decision was clear, easy. This time, everything had changed. Nothing was easy. Nothing was clear.

Grace awakened with a pounding headache. She knew the headache was caused by a concussion she received in an automobile accident. Aside from her name, that was the only thing she knew. And she only knew those two things because the hospital staff had told her. Otherwise, her mind was completely blank. Blank. Empty. She didn't even know her own birthday. Slowly, carefully, she opened her eyelids and the first thing she focused on was an incredibly handsome man who was sound asleep on the chair beside her bed. Unruly dark, wavy hair framed his strong face. High cheekbones and a stubborn chin almost overpowered his full, perfect mouth. His eyes were closed, but she'd bet they were brown. He simply had the coloring for it. One black curl fell to his forehead.

Suddenly he opened his eyes, and for several seconds he and Grace stared at each other. Looking into his fathomless black orbs, wave after wave of feeling washed over Grace. She loved him. Even without knowing who he was, Grace knew she loved him. She knew they'd been intimate, as close as two people could be. There were deep feelings between them. They'd been through a lot together. And not all of it was happy.

Finally, he said, "Hello, Grace."

She swallowed. "Hello."

Obviously seeing her fear, he smiled. "If the expression

on your face is anything to go by, I'd say the doctor was right. You really have lost your memory."

She shook her head sadly. "I don't know who you are."

"Then I guess I should tell you."

She nodded.

This time *he* swallowed. When he spoke, it was slowly. "I'm your husband." He paused, then added, "Nick Spinelli."

Grace couldn't help noticing that he seemed to be watching for her reaction, and it confirmed part of what she'd felt when she'd stared into his eyes. Not everything she'd been through with this man was happy.

When she'd awakened in the emergency room and the doctor told her that her husband had been called, she remembered the quick stab of fear she'd felt. A lesser version of that fear had resurfaced now, but she also had an indescribable urge to hold him, to cling to him like a lifeline. The conflicting feelings didn't make any kind of sense. In fact, they made about as much sense as the bubble of giddy delight that threatened to make her laugh because her husband was so good-looking.

He caught her attention again. "Did Dr. Ringer explain that you'd been in an accident?"

Grace nodded.

"I hoped he had. He told me your only real injury is a concussion. He also told me your memory loss is normal because of that concussion."

Grace settled back on her pillow. Labeling her nameless fears and conflicting reactions typical paranoia resulting from not having any recollection of herself or her life, Grace had to admit things weren't as bad they could be. Nick Spinelli seemed like a normal, average man, which probably meant *she* was an ordinary person, too. She wasn't a bank robber, a hooker or even a housewife trapped in a bad marriage.

At least she didn't think so.

"So, how long have we been married?"

He grinned at her. "Would you believe it's been ten years?"

"I'd believe anything," Grace said, then laughed slightly. "You could probably tell me anything right now and get away with it. So, if there's an excuse you need to try out on me, this is your chance."

He drew a long breath and said, "No. No excuses." Changing the subject, he bounced from his seat and busied himself with her pillows. "Do you want me to call the nurse or something? It's been hours since anyone's been in to check on you."

Clucking her tongue, Grace shook her head. "How would you know? You were sleeping. When I woke up, you were so dead to the world a brass band could have marched through and you wouldn't have noticed."

He looked at her. For a good ten seconds he stared at her as if he hadn't expected her to make that kind of comment, then he grinned foolishly. "Yeah, I guess you're right."

"Of course I'm right," she said, though she heaved a resigned sigh. "But you're also right. I think we should call the nurse to see if I'm allowed to have an aspirin or something. My head is killing me."

Her simple statement seemed to panic him and he fumbled for the call button that hung on the side rail of her bed. He dropped it twice. The second time it landed on her arm. He scooped it up, and as he did so, the back of his fingers brushed across her breast. His breath came out in a loud gasp, but he acted as if nothing had happened. Instead, he depressed the switch, dropped the call button and quickly walked to the window where he opened the blinds.

Grace narrowed her eyes at him. She could understand his being nervous because she'd been hurt. She could also understand his being nervous because she'd lost her memory. But she couldn't understand why her own husband would jump simply because he'd touched her. "So, tell me about our life."

Smiling a little too brightly, he turned to face her. "What do you want to know?"

She felt it again. Not the force of fear that she'd experienced the night before, but a swift gust of woman's intuition like the one she got when she'd first looked into his eyes moments ago. The one that told her something was wrong.

Uneasy, she asked, "What do I do for a living?"

"You're an accountant," Nick answered immediately because that was what she'd planned to study in college. For the first time since he'd allowed himself to get involved in this problem, he realized this wasn't merely a matter of being nice to her for the next two weeks. Pretending to be her husband was going to be much more complicated than that. First, he didn't know anything about her life. Second, he couldn't help her regain her memory because anything he told her would be speculation or fabrication—except the past. Which was something he really didn't care to remember...

"Where do we live?"

That he could handle. "Outskirts of Turner. Only about ten minutes away from here."

"Really?"

"Really."

"Do we have a nice house?"

"We have an incredible home," Nick said and meant it. "It's a log cabin nestled in a mountain. Our closest neighbor is a bear," he said and was rewarded by her giggle. "Our house is three stories, with two decks connected by a wooden stairway in the back that looks like a great big Z. We have sliding glass doors that let in sunshine in the morning and breezes in the afternoon."

"Sounds pretty nice."

"It is. It's great."

"Do I have any family other than you?"

"Oh, heavens, yes," Nick said. "You have a brother Cal. Your parents died when you were young, but you were adopted by a man named Angus MacFarland. He's big, he's rowdy and he's very, very rich."

That made her smile. "He is?"

"Yes. But you never wanted his money. You're determined to make your own way in the world."

She sighed with relief. "That's good."

Nick waited a minute, studied her face, then said, "Any of this bringing *anything* back?"

"No. Nothing."

Just then, the nurse arrived, and Nick walked to the window again. All in all, this wasn't going too badly, but he felt a surge of guilt because what was good for him—her lost memory—wasn't good for Grace. He didn't want to continually hope she didn't remember, but he didn't want to confront the past, either.

After giving Grace something for her headache, taking her temperature and blood pressure and asking her a few routine questions, the nurse left.

Nick turned to look at her and she smiled. "Now that you say we're married, I can see our marriage certificate, of all things, in my head."

Nick wasn't about to tell her that was because she'd had it on the front seat of her car. Not only could that upset her, which the doctor had warned him against, but he wasn't ready to deal with the questions it would raise. Like why was their marriage certificate sitting on the front seat of her car? Had she come to Turner seeking a divorce? Or was she here simply to ask him why he'd never gotten the divorce as he'd promised?

He wasn't really sure about that himself. Once he started his own business and had his mother settled in

Dallas, money was no longer the issue it had been in the beginning, when he could hardly afford to eat, let alone to get an attorney.

With his newly acquired wealth, his marriage to Grace was the only piece of his past he didn't settle. He wasn't foolish enough to think he didn't get the divorce because he wanted her back. Even if he'd wanted her back, he knew she'd never have him. And he wouldn't blame her. Though he felt he'd had no choice but to leave her the way he did, leaving without speaking to her had been cruel. She had every right to hate him.

He wouldn't deprive her of that.

"I need to run home to shower, shave and pick up a few things," Nick said as he walked toward the door. "Why don't you try to get some rest?"

No, he wouldn't deprive her of that.

Chapter Three

Jogging up the flight of steps to the second floor of the medical center, Nick sighed heavily, feeling guilty again because he was relieved Grace couldn't remember him.

Sorting through everything after he left her last night, he recognized that what bothered him the most about being face-to-face with his wife once more was that Grace had every right in the world to be furious with him. She had deserved for Nick to tell her that he was leaving. She'd also deserved an explanation for *why* he was leaving. But he'd chickened out.

After deciding that Grace should go to the hospital without him, Nick's drive to his parents' home was short and uneventful. But the instant he pulled up to the house, he could sense trouble.

For thirty seconds, he sat as still as a mouse, listening to the rustle of the grasslands around him, and he debated not going in. But when he heard his mother's scream, instinct propelled him off the bike, up the steps and through the open front door.

"I've told you a thousand times," Jake Spinelli shouted

at his wife who huddled pitifully against the sofa, her arms shielding her face. "...to have this house clean when I get home, and instead what do I find? A pigsty!"

Nick stopped his father's tirade with one spontaneous right hook to the jaw. His father's head snapped back and for a few seconds Nick actually wondered if the punch hadn't sobered him. But Jake shook his head as if to clear a haze and, when he looked at his son, his eyes gleamed with the thirst for revenge and the aftereffects of liquor.

"Don't, Pop," Nick said, keeping the pleading out of his voice because he was sick of it. He hadn't expected to hit his dad. He hadn't wanted to. He really hadn't ever wanted to hit anyone...ever. The pain that seared his knuckles and tingled up his arm wasn't satisfying. It was sickening. But that punch was purely spontaneous. He hadn't thought about it, he'd simply done it. And he'd done it because he was sick to death of everything. He couldn't take the punches, the shouting, the abuse anymore!

Which was why he was moving to California.

"Come on, Pop, just sit down. I'll help Mom clean up the place after supper."

His father acted as if he hadn't heard him. "You think you can take me, boy?" he sneered, his voice tinged with laughter.

"No, I don't think I can take you," Nick said dully as he turned and began to walk away. If he was lucky, his father would let him go. If he wasn't, God only knew what would happen.

"Then stay the hell out of my business," Jake said, his voice a hoarse whisper.

"You can count on that," Nick said and prayed that Angus would be well enough that Nick and Grace could leave in the morning. "Come on, Mom," he softly entreated, holding out his hand to help his mother rise. "We'll go in the kitchen and make supper."

"Damn right you will," Jake muttered as Nick led his mother into the kitchen.

He pulled her to the sink where he started the cool water running, then he grabbed a clean cloth and a tray of ice and created a makeshift ice pack. "Put this on your cheek. I'll make some eggs or something."

Nick's mother nodded absently, though she managed a weak smile. Nick smiled back at her, but guilt stabbed at him. He didn't want to leave her alone, he didn't. But he also knew he couldn't stay.

"You shouldn't have hit your pop today," Wanda Spinelli said.

He glanced at her. "I wasn't going to stand by and do nothing while he smacked you around."

"That's just the point," Wanda said. "He wasn't about to hit me anymore. And I think you might have made things worse."

"He's not hitting you now, is he?"

"No."

"Then I didn't make things worse."

"Not tonight," Wanda conceded quietly.

Cracking an egg against a black skillet, Nick vented his fury. But when he spoke, his words were every bit as calm and quiet as his mother's. "I know what you're saying," he admitted as if they were talking about the weather or his grades instead of the fact that his father regularly drank too much then used his mother as an outlet for his anger.

"Then you know what you have to do."

Nick squeezed his eyes shut. She *wanted* him to leave. Despite the sense of futility that swamped him, he calmly said, "Yeah, actually, I pretty much figured it out last year. I was only waiting for high school graduation."

"That was two weeks ago," Wanda said worriedly and Nick suppressed a heavy sigh. To hear her, anyone would think she was anxious to get her son out of the house because *he* was the problem.

"Yeah, but Grace needed some time to settle her life." He paused, considered, then added, "We got married yesterday."

"You did!"

It was the first time in years Nick could remember hearing his mother's voice sounding young and happy.

He grinned at her. "Yeah, we did."

"Oh, Nick, that's wonderful…"

"Oh, Nick, that's wonderful," Jake mocked from the kitchen doorway. "What a pathetic sap you are," he said as he stumbled to the refrigerator for another beer. "You think that rich bitch really wants you?"

Deciding to ignore his father, Nick flipped the eggs.

Unfortunately, his mother answered. "And why wouldn't she?" Wanda said, unexpectedly defending Nick. "Look at him, he's as handsome as you were, Jake. And he's smart and he's going to go to college. Why wouldn't she want him?"

For a few seconds, Jake said nothing, only stared at Nick. Then he lifted his beer to his mouth and took a long swallow. After wiping the back of his hand across his lips, he said, "You know, you're right. Why *wouldn't* she want him? Our boy's as good as any of those MacFarland kids. None of 'em's his, you know. The only one he adopted was the girl. They're all misfits. Kids nobody else wanted. Not one of them's any better than we are."

Nick didn't have to hear the rest to know where this conversation was leading. Fear built in his chest, but he squelched it, snapped off the gas burner of the stove, and quickly deposited the eggs onto a waiting dish. "Here, have some dinner," he said casually, sliding the plate on the table in front of his father.

Jake shoved the plate away. "I don't want this slop! I

want to eat what MacFarland eats. And why the hell shouldn't I? My son is married to his daughter.''

The terror in Nick's chest expanded painfully. Every fear he ever had about his father came to life, personified in that one short discourse.

''In fact, I think you and I should go over there tonight, Wanda. Go fix yourself up—''

''You can't go over tonight,'' Nick quickly interrupted. ''Angus is in the hospital. He had a heart attack.''

Jake grinned wickedly. ''Yeah, probably after he found out his daughter had married you.'' He paused long enough to chuckle drunkenly. ''But don't worry, boy,'' he added, winking superiorly. ''I won't let you hang out to dry, here. I'll visit MacFarland. Have a man-to-man talk. Make everything okay for you.''

''*You* can't make everything okay for me,'' Nick shouted, though he had intended to keep his cool. ''If you go over there all you'll do is screw things up...''

Jake rose, shoving his chair behind him. ''You ashamed of me, boy?''

Hell, yes! Nick wanted to say. He said, ''No, Pop. You know I'm not.'' Then, hoping his father was drunk enough to be easily confused, he added, ''But the truth is I didn't marry Grace yet. I only told Mom I *wanted* to marry Grace. I'm going to California. Grace doesn't want to come with me. So we can't get married.''

Jake's eyes narrowed. ''Who do you think you're playing with here?'' he asked angrily. ''I know what I heard, and I see what you're doing. You don't want me and your mama associating with your wife's kin...''

Wild with fury, Nick spun on his father. ''I told you, she's not my wife! And you stay the hell away from her!''

He left then, his boots tapping on the planks as he ran down the wooden steps. That was it. The final straw. He had to get the hell out of this town, away from his father, and it had to be *now*.

Nick drove to the hospital and headed for Angus MacFarland's room. As he suspected, Angus's bed was surrounded. Grace sat on the edge and Cal and Ryan Kelly, the third child Angus raised, stood on the opposite side. Nick didn't really want to go inside, so he waited until he caught Cal's attention. Cal surreptitiously nudged Grace and she came out into the hall.

"What are you doing here?" Grace whispered, as if trying to keep Angus from hearing.

Nick cleared his throat. "My dad and I had a fight tonight."

Grace clutched her throat. "Oh, my God. What happened?"

"Actually, Grace, he was drunk…" Nick said, but he stopped himself. He didn't *want* her to know this. Just like he didn't want his father to barge into her life, he didn't want Grace to see this side of his. He kept all this from her for four years, and he had no intention of telling her any of it now.

"He had a little too much to drink," Nick said, amending his story. "We got into an argument over dinner and I left."

"Oh, that's too bad," Grace said, relieved in a way that was so beautifully naive that Nick felt almost weak with relief that she didn't question any further. "But I'm sure you'll clear everything up before we leave for California," she said, straightening the collar of Nick's black leather jacket. "I'm looking forward to meeting your family. In fact, I thought we could stay with them when we came home at Christmas, and then we could all go over to Angus's for Christmas Eve supper."

Nick could see it. Clearly, vividly, he could see his father whining and whimpering and begging to Angus MacFarland. But more than that, he could feel the heat of embarrassment and humiliation he'd face because his father would get stone drunk. Worse, he could see the look of horror on Grace's face the first time she saw one of his father's tirades. And even worse, he could finally see that he had put Grace in danger by making her part of his family. When his father was sober, he was only a whining loser. When he was drunk, Jake Spinelli didn't care whom he hit or why.

Because their plan had always been to get married and leave, Nick never realized that marriage meant drawing Grace into his life and he didn't want her there. Not only to protect her, but to protect himself from the humiliation. How could he tell the woman he loved that he lived with the fear of being beaten every day, or that he never knew where his dinner was coming from, or that he paid for the groceries with what little money he made on the weekends because his father drank his pay—when and if he worked. Could he tell Grace the countless number of times their electricity had been turned off? Could he admit they no longer had phone service? Could he handle the shame of admitting how he'd really lived all these years she thought he was so wonderful...?

He couldn't.

"Look, Grace," he said, stepping away from her. "I gotta go."

She smiled. "Okay. I'll see you later."

Nick looked at his shoes. "Yeah. I'll see you later."

He knew he should have had the courage to tell Grace face-to-face that their marriage had been a mistake, but he didn't. Instead, he rode his bike home and told his mother that he hadn't really married Grace, and if his father woke up thinking he had, all he had to do was call the ranch and he'd see Grace was still there. Then he wrote Grace a note telling her he was leaving and that he'd handle the divorce, slipped it in Grace's ranch mail box, and left for California on his motorcycle.

Alone. Just like he suspected he would always be.

Oh, he'd told himself that he couldn't stay in Crossroads Creek one more night or the situation between himself and his father would have escalated out of control, and he'd probably been right. But he still could have snuck over to the Triple Moors and spoken with Grace the same way he had a thousand times since the ninth grade. He could have thrown pebbles at her window. She would have crept down the stairs, met him on the porch and dashed to the privacy of their favorite tree, where they could have talked for hours if they'd needed to.

But he hadn't. At eighteen he hadn't had the courage to admit the reasons why he'd left. At eighteen he wasn't mature enough to face the humiliation of revealing how he'd lived. At eighteen he wasn't strong enough to endure the disappointment in her eyes.

So he owed her, and he was repaying her by staying with her until she was able to go home again or until Angus could come and get her. If she got her memory back between now and then, he'd worry about the repercussions and ramifications when they hit.

But, despite all his brave talk, Nick thought, shoving open the door to her room, he hoped he wasn't about to face those repercussions and ramifications now.

"Hi," he said, catching her attention as he stepped through the door.

Her bed had been raised enough that she was sitting. Someone on the hospital staff must have given her a magazine because she was leafing through one. Her thick sable hair had been neatly combed, but, Nick noticed, she really hadn't changed the style much from when they were younger. Nearly shoulder length and full of luxurious body that caused a slight inward curve at the bottom, her hair was styled exactly as it had been for her senior picture—a picture he still carried in his wallet.

"Hi," she said.

"How do you feel today?" he asked cheerily as he walked to her bed. When he'd returned the day before, she'd been sleeping soundly. She was still asleep when he'd left last night. Seeing her sitting up was a welcome sign.

"Like someone ran over me with a truck."

Nick couldn't help it, he smiled. He was glad she hadn't lost her irreverent sense of humor. It was one of the things he had loved about her. "Then I think you're progressing exactly on schedule. Last night while you were sleeping, the doctor told me you'd find bumps and bruises you didn't know you had, and it sounds like you did."

"What's in the bag?"

"A nightgown, toothbrush and your perfume," Nick answered casually. He'd found the things in the suitcase the sheriff had given him. He'd also seen she brought a pair of jeans, a sweater, two T-shirts and a business suit.

"Oh, wonderful!" Grace gasped happily. "They say the sense of smell is the best way to stimulate memory. If this is the perfume I wear all the time, I'm liable to take one whiff and be myself again."

She reached for the bag and Nick experienced a moment of panic. The minute she got her memory back, she wouldn't like him anymore. He had reconciled himself to the fact that she would be angry and he would deserve it, but the thought that he didn't want to lose her so quickly brought him up short. He refused to give in to the urge to withhold the perfume, and, instead, reached over and pulled the bottle from the bag, reminding him̶̶̶ ̶̶̶that having her in his life was a complication he d̶̶̶ ̶̶̶

He spritzed a quick spray into the roo̶̶̶ ̶̶̶d her eyes and inhaled deeply. She smile̶̶̶ flowery scent hit her nostrils, but ̶̶̶ open, Nick knew the scent hadn't̶̶̶

Unfortunately, it did awaken̶̶̶ right back to their one night t̶̶̶ Grace had worn a beautiful̶̶̶ fume, the aroma that was̶̶̶

He inhaled again.

They'd taken a room in a small, questionable motel in Vegas, and Nick gallantly gave Grace the bathroom first. He remembered trying to be nonchalant about the whole deal, but inside, his nerves were jumping. He experienced the usual fears that all men have, but he had an extra set of apprehensions because this was Grace...*Grace*. She was the first person to talk with him as if he was an equal. She was the first woman to flirt with him. She was the first woman to use her feminine powers to make him realize he had masculine powers. Up to that point, everything had worked right, everything had gone right. After every make-out session she'd seemed to like him more. They'd seemed to have gotten closer. He'd felt like more of a man.

Their wedding night was the ultimate test.

Nervous, uncertain, he'd fought to keep from prowling the bedroom, but when Grace came out of the bathroom, looking like an ethereal vision in her white cloudlike nightie, instinct kicked in. When they tumbled to the bed together and he pressed his face into her neck, and got a whiff of her wonderful scent, he wondered why he'd worried. They weren't experienced, but what they lacked in actual knowledge they made up for in genuine emotion—affection. God, how he'd loved her.

He remembered thinking they were made for each other.

"What did I do wrong?"

Her question snapped Nick out of his reverie and he cleared his throat. "I'm sorry. What did you say?"

Grace gazed at him, her expression both confused and awestruck. "You were giving me such an odd look, I ____ I must have done something stupid while I had ____osed."

____" Nick said, brushing off the whole epi-____tion threw him for a loop. If she remembered him, if she remembered what had happened between them, that's exactly what she might be asking— probably what she had every right to ask. He got the crazy need to reassure her and he smiled. "You didn't do anything wrong."

"I also didn't remember anything."

"The doctor said you weren't supposed to push yourself, and he said not to expect too much. Let's not make a big deal out of this."

She sighed. "That's easy for you to say. You know who I am. You remember me. I don't remember you."

"Do you feel uncomfortable with me?"

"No." She paused, caught his gaze. "At least not in the way I think you mean."

"Then how?"

"I just feel strange knowing you know things about me, when I couldn't even remember your name."

Touched by the sad tone in her voice, he sat on the edge of the bed, trying to give her a sense of intimacy and companionship without going too far. "What would you like to know?" he asked softly.

She looked him right in the eye. "Anything."

"Okay," he said, then took her hand and clasped it between both of his. "My name is Nick Spinelli and we met in high school. Ninth grade."

Settling back against her pillow, Grace smiled slightly, but she never released his gaze, as if measuring his words for honesty. Which didn't bother him. He _____ ll her many, many things without ever once lyi___

"I was this rough-and-tumble rebel ___ _____ _Angus MacFarland's_ daughter. The s___ ___ envied and all the boys wanted to ___ is rich."

Her smile grew. "So you've ___

"I didn't marry you beca___ Nick said quickly, but not ___

was defending himself. He wanted her to understand that he'd loved her for *her*. "I married you because you were beautiful and smart, and because of how you made me feel about myself."

That seemed to confuse her. "How did I make you feel about yourself?"

Awkward though it was, Nick continued to look her in the eye. "Actually, Grace, you made me feel like a man."

"Oh," she said and unexpectedly shifted from her pillow until she was leaning against him.

Understanding that she was frightened and confused and that her movement indicated that newborn trust had coupled with her touching need of support, he lifted his arm until he could wrap it around her shoulders, allowing her to snuggle against his side. She needed him. That's all that mattered now. He didn't allow himself to consider that what he was doing might be dangerous to his own heart and emotions. He was too busy remembering that though she hadn't known it, in many of *his* hours of need, Grace had been there for him. Now, he would reciprocate by being here for her.

"Tell me more."

"Well, like I said," Nick said, then scooted up on the bed until they were both more comfortable. "I was this rough-and-tumble rebel sort, and everybody was more or less afraid of me. I wanted it that way because I was the new kid in school and I was proving myself."

"Did it work?"

"Oh, yeah, for a good three years most of the kids in the school walked on the other side of the hall just to make sure they didn't accidentally make me mad."

She giggled. "You're making that up."

"No kidding," he said then crossed his heart. "Grace, groove here. I was a teenage boy. It was better en liked."

ked, looking up at him.

"See that?" he said, then tipped her chin. "You must be getting your memory back because you didn't believe me then, either."

When she didn't answer, but searched his eyes, Nick got the suspicion that he'd just made the biggest mistake of his life. It wasn't so much how she looked to him, but how she looked at him that sent all his senses screaming. Her beautiful violet eyes were dark with concern, but there was an innate trust very visible in them. She believed every word he said, but she was searching for more...for everything. Just as she always had when they were younger. Everything about her was precisely as it was ten years ago. She might be older, she might be a company president, or a government official, or a check-out girl at the supermarket, for all he knew, but the way she was looking at him now was exactly as she'd looked at him all those years ago. With trust. With the expectation of perfection. And with, probably, undeserved love. Everything was so much the same, he felt as if he'd fallen through a time warp.

His gaze roved down and settled on her lips. Raspberry red, plump and kissable, her lips had been the object of many of his late-night fantasies. Even knowing her taste, her scent, and even what she felt like in places he was sure no one else had touched, it was her lips that tempted him beyond reason.

Ten years later, he felt the resonating nee̶ ̶ clearly as if he were eighteen again, and he wonder̶ ̶̶ ̶issed her, would she taste as sweet?

As if uncomfortable under his scrut̶ broke the spell. "If you thought it w̶ than liked, how did you and I ever̶

Knowing he'd dodged a bullet̶ he wasn't happy about that, Ni̶ you didn't believe me."

She grinned. "I sound s̶

"Not stubborn, but definitely your own woman."

"Good," she said, settling against him again. "What else?"

He thought for a few seconds. "Well, you tried your hand at ranching for a while. Against Angus's wishes, you went out on the range with your brother Cal and Ryan Kelly..." He slanted her a look. "Ryan is another boy raised by Angus," he explained. "But though you loved the riding and being outdoors, you missed your books, and within two weeks you were permanently positioned in the library again."

"Why is it I get the impression you fit in there somewhere?"

He smiled. Her memory might be gone but there was nothing wrong with her intuition. "Because I did. When everyone was out on ranch business, you could sneak away. We'd meet at one of three different places, depending upon where the ranch hands were working that day, and we'd hang out..." *Make out,* Nick amended in his head. They would lie on a blanket for hours and kiss. Kiss, touch and drive each other to the brink of insanity.

"Hang out?" Grace echoed, confused. "We'd just sort of sit there?"

Nick shifted uncomfortably. This was the last thing he needed to be remembering right now. He didn't have the right to want to kiss her. They weren't really husband and wife in the conventional sense of the word, but more than that he'd deserted her. If she had her memory back, she wouldn't be sitting beside him, let alone inadvertently enticing him into talking about kissing.

"We didn't really just *sit* there."

"Then what did we do?"

"Well, we did stuff."

"what stuff?"

teenage kids usually do when their parents

"You're losing me."

God help him, he was going to have to say it, and in saying it he'd see it, and in seeing it he'd experience it, if only in his mind. And remembering would whet his already awakened appetite. Exasperated, Nick sighed. "Grace, we used to lie on a blanket in the woods and neck."

"Oh," Grace said, feeling her face flame with color. Her back-and-forth reactions to Nick were driving her crazy. First, she felt overwhelming love counteracted by the fact that she didn't know him. A torrent of trust came second, but piercing through that was the constant reminder that you couldn't—*shouldn't*—trust someone you didn't remember. Now she was being pummeled by a fierce attraction, and all the while her logical self screamed that she shouldn't be attracted to someone who was little more than a stranger, even if he claimed to be her husband. The conflicting emotions bombarding her were pulling her apart. Strong instinct drew her toward him, while sound logic dragged her away.

And through it all, she couldn't help wondering why her husband hadn't kissed her. He hadn't kissed her hello. He hadn't kissed her goodbye. He never kissed her because he was glad to see her, or even glad to see she was alive, considering she'd been in a serious accident. Worse, the one time she thought he might kiss her, he'd debated it so long she knew he wasn't going to. She had the suspicion that even holding her hadn't been in his plan. It almost seemed that, if he'd had his way, he wouldn't have touched her at all. The only question was

Still snuggled against his side, she l
He picked that precise second to glanc
knew her question was evident in h
tion didn't hold a candle to the tho
having. She could see that som
It could have been hope fighti

condition. It could have been desire battling concern for her well-being. She didn't know. She couldn't tell. But something was definitely troubling him.

After that, he got off the bed and took them away from revisiting the past, telling her she'd had enough memories for one day and that she needed to rest her brain. He kept her busy by engaging her in an uncomplicated game of rummy. He arranged for her to have television in her room, helped her choose her menu for the next day and even consulted with the doctor when he came into her room, but he stayed away from her bed. He left her room only to buy lunch, and then to buy dinner, but though physically he was with her through the entire day, mentally, or maybe emotionally, he kept himself a good arm's distance.

Now, ten minutes before the end of visiting hours, she watched him carefully. He was beginning to prowl again. Roaming her room as if something was dreadfully wrong. In her good assessment, he was worried about her, considerate about her sensitivity to not having any recollection of her husband and dying to kiss her—if only because he missed her.

In her bad assessment, something was wrong. Something was terribly, terribly wrong.

Five minutes before the end of visiting hours, he plucked his leather jacket from the back of the plastic chair. Trying to be casual, he glanced at his watch. Grace could swear she saw sweat beading on his upper lip.

Three minutes before the end of visiting hours, he slid into his coat. He took a nervous breath before he began clucking about the arrangement of her pillows and visiting the nurses' station to make sure the night staff would take proper care of her.

A minute before the end of visiting hours, he started

to contracted painfully. He was going to

leave without kissing her, and she still hadn't determined if all this nervousness was because he didn't want to hurt her, or because he didn't want to kiss her.

Not even realizing she was probably the boldest woman on the planet, she drew a long breath. "Nicki," she entreated softly, calling him the nickname without thinking. "Are you going to leave without kissing me goodbye?"

Chapter Four

It was the nickname that did it.

Heat suffused him and he could swear they were back by the river, one of the three places they used to meet. He felt eighteen again. Not in all the horrible, god-awful ways memories of his father brought, but in all the good, all the very, very good ways Grace made him feel.

He faced her and gave her the line he'd practiced all afternoon. "I don't want to hurt you."

She smiled. "You'll hurt me more if you don't kiss me."

Her words went directly to his heart. He remembered her as young, eager and sometimes scared, but always open and receptive because she trusted him. He remembered himself as young, even more eager and in some ways even more scared because she trusted him so much. And he realized at that moment that nothing had really changed.

"Come here," she said, holding out her arms.

Common sense warred with healthy curiosity and pure, unadulterated desire. If he kissed her, he'd be opening the doors to problems he couldn't even begin to count they were so vast. If he didn't, she wouldn't trust him. His presence wouldn't help her...and, he'd hurt her.

He couldn't bear the thought of hurting her. Not again. Not this way. Not when the alternative to hurting her was so easy, so tempting.

Taking a silent breath for strength and courage, he walked to her bed. She held his gaze with a hopeful, gentle stare that prompted him forward. If it ended up that he hurt her again by kissing her, the devil would surely take his soul for this. But that was only if he hurt her by kissing her. If she got her memory back, she'd remember him deserting her so well and so clearly she'd probably forget this one little kiss. And if he would be damned to hell for anything, it would be the time it had taken to mend the broken heart he gave her when he left her the day after he married her.

He leaned down, into her open arms, and felt the blissful sensation of having her envelope him in waiting warmth. Still holding her gaze, he pressed his mouth to hers, watching as the lids of her eyes drifted closed. The smooth softness of her lips started a slow, heavy pounding of his heart, then she opened her mouth beneath his and he felt himself being pulled into a vortex of sensation that begged him to forget logic and reason and follow where this led.

He silenced his conscience and took what she offered.

She was nothing if not generous. She gave him everything he sought, everything he wanted, and suggested more. If it weren't for the discomfort of bending down beside a bed, Nick knew he would have been hard-pressed to stop from taking everything. But he was bent beside her bed and he genuinely believed that was God's way of keeping him sane and reminding him he didn't have the right to take the kiss he'd taken, let alone try for more.

He pulled away. "Good night, Grace."

Looking content, she sank against her pillow. "Good night, Nick."

The next morning when Nick arrived in her room, Grace knew with absolute certainty that she loved him. In fact, she'd be willing to bet her father's fortune that she didn't merely love Nick Spinelli, she adored him. Solid and honest, breathtakingly handsome and very male, yet endearingly vulnerable, Nick Spinelli was too perfect for her not to love.

When their eyes met as he walked through her hospital-room door that morning, Grace decided she'd also be willing to bet the huge fortune of the father she couldn't remember that Nick loved her, too. Or at least he had at one time.

When he didn't kiss her hello, the seeds of doubt that had been planted the day before started to grow. When he jerked back as if she'd burned him just because she touched his arm to get his attention, those seeds began to sprout. When he forgot himself and nearly brushed the hair from her forehead, as if that would have been his natural response but he couldn't give in to instinct any-more, Grace's seeds were nearly a beanstalk.

"Can I ask you a question?"

Looking like a man who'd escaped a fate worse than death because he'd caught himself before he touched her, Nick turned from the window to face her. If he opened or closed the blinds any more than he already had, the people in the building across the street would think he was sending Morse code. "Sure. Anything."

"Why aren't you at work?"

Because her question was so innocent, Nick visibly relaxed again. "I'm off for six weeks."

"Wow, some vacation."

"No vacation. I simply don't have an assignment."

Her eyebrows rose in interest. "You don't have an assignment? What are you, a spy?"

He laughed. "No. No spy. But you may not be too thrilled when you do discover my occupation."

"Now you have me curious."

He drew a long breath. "I'm a corporate killer."

"A corporate killer?" she asked, confused. "You kill companies?"

Nick laughed heartily. "No, I usually just fire the president and most of the senior management and bring in new blood."

Falling against her pillow, Grace sighed. "You're right. I don't like it. That sounds absolutely heartless."

"It is. That's why I need big rests in between assignments."

Thinking him the sweetest, most sensitive man in the world, Grace asked, "How the heck did *you* ever get into a profession like that?"

Nick knew he'd ended up in this job because he was a loner. A quick learner and even quicker thinker, he could go into a company and in two weeks diagnose its troubles. He could tell you who worked and who didn't. He could tell you whose work was productive and whose wasn't. But a lot of people could do that. It took the personality of a loner, somebody who saw the good and the bad and who could, without emotion, keep the good and get rid of the bad, to really be effective at turning a company around for its stockholders.

None of that explanation seemed too difficult or too personal to give to Grace unless you realized she'd undoubtedly ask him about how or why he was a loner. Though he'd more or less revealed that when he told her about high school, the truth was, he didn't care to expand upon it. That would mean he'd have to reveal that he hadn't changed much since high school, and, worse, to explain why.

He skirted the truth. "I worked for a company that was about to go under. I knew it. The board of directors knew it. The people from the board who worked for the company didn't have guts enough to face the truth. The people from the board who didn't work for the company knew they had no choice. I was a senior accountant..."

"You're an accountant," she gasped. "Just like me."

In order that she wouldn't think about that too long, he dismissed its significance with a nod. "Because I was a senior accountant, one of the board members approached me privately. I gave him my assessment of the situation and it ended up that I was a hundred percent right."

"So, if you turned the company around, why didn't they just make you president of that company?"

He couldn't really tell her that he'd enjoyed bringing new life to something that was dying, and that after all was said and done, it was hard to go back to being an employee when he now craved the excitement of that kind of challenge. That was too personal, too private.

After their kiss from the day before, he knew that if he wanted to walk away from this woman with his heart even somewhat intact, he was going to have to give her more facts and less emotion. Physically, she was absolute perfection to him. He was so sexually attracted to her, he had difficulty keeping himself sane in the same room with her. If he started revealing his deepest, most personal thoughts, he'd be so in love with her by the time she got her memory back, he'd never forget her a second time.

He stuck to the facts.

"The board member who originally approached me was a director for several big companies. That was six years ago, right around the time when everybody was downsizing, and he saw I could serve his purposes much better by going from business to business, doing a little preliminary undercover work as an employee and eventually giving him a report on what needed changing. I did so well, he kept pushing me from one company to the next until eventually I called him, told him I was going into business for myself and quoted a flat fee for the next assignment that would have made another person's eyes bulge.''

Grace laughed lightly. "What happened?"

"Much like your adoptive father, Angus, George Neuman didn't even bat an eye. He told me he knew a good thing when he saw it and simply gave me the name of the personnel director for the next company he wanted me to 'hit.' I used his name as a reference, got the job, and we went on as we had been for the two years before, except now I was getting paid a hell of a lot more.''

She studied him for several seconds. "So, now *you're* rich.''

"Don't read too much into that,'' Nick said, if only because there was plenty that could be read into it and most of it would be right. He was tired of being poor, damn sick and tired of being poor. When he found his strength he exploited it. And though he couldn't rival Angus MacFarland in wealth, he was far, far beyond comfortable.

"So where do *I* work?''

The question took him so much by surprise that Nick had to stop the puzzled expression from forming on his face. Knowing he couldn't think for more than twenty seconds without arousing her suspicions, he smiled and said, "You work for me.''

The very thought appealed to him since they actually would make an excellent team, and he couldn't stop a smug grin. It was a perfect answer. Because he ran his own company, with limited employees and limited customers, he could answer any question she had without having to think too hard.

"Am I good?''

"You're very good,'' Nick said, realizing that, also,

would be true. When he knew her in high school, she was patient, thorough and tireless in her quest for perfection. "I do most of the legwork, and the nasty stuff like firing people. You're pretty much behind the scenes."

Grace didn't know why, but that sounded off to her. She could believe she worked for him, but for some reason she didn't feel like a "behind the scenes" person.

Before she could question Nick about it, though, the door of the hospital room opened. The dietary technician entered with her lunch tray. "Hello, Mrs. Spinelli," she happily greeted. "Where would you like this?"

"I'll get it," Nick said, immediately jumping to the young woman's aid. He took the tray from her hands and set it on Grace's bed table.

"Thanks," the girl said, smiling shyly. "Do you have your menu for tomorrow?"

"Right here," Nick said, handing it over.

"It's funny," Grace said after the dietary aide had gone. "I have no memory of you at all, but I know with absolute certainty that I hate carrots." She looked down at her tray with dismay.

Nick laughed. "You *do* hate carrots."

"And what else?" Grace asked, occupying them both while she tried to find something on the tray she could eat.

"Well, you always hated the Ruzkowski twins."

"The Ruzkowski twins?"

"Two freckle-faced redheads who eventually went on to become doctors."

"Hmm," Grace said, realizing that hadn't helped her memory one bit and also realizing there wasn't one bite of food on her tray she could eat. Though she wasn't sure how, she knew she wasn't a picky eater. Still, she obviously had some standards. Using her fork, she moved some very dry-looking peas around her plate.

"You're not eating," Nick observed softly. "You're playing with your food."

She swallowed. "I know. There just isn't anything here I feel like eating."

Even Grace heard the melancholy in her voice. She wasn't surprised when Nick sat on the edge of the bed again. "I know this is hard," he said, seemingly searching for something that would help her cope. "I can't imagine what it would be like not to have any memory."

"You also can't imagine what it's like to have to eat this food," Grace joked because she didn't want him feeling sorry for her.

When he laughed, she knew she'd accomplished her purposes. "You're right. I don't because I go to the restaurant across the street for lunch and dinner. So," he said, grabbing her tray and dumping the contents, plastic plate and all, into the trash can by the door, "what do you say I run across the street and get some takeout for both of us?"

Grace's lips involuntarily bowed into a smile. "You mean it?"

"I mean it."

"You don't mind?"

"Of course I don't mind. It'll take me twenty minutes."

It actually took him thirty-five, but Grace didn't care. When he displayed a hot turkey sandwich and mashed potatoes smothered in rich gravy, she could have kissed him. Even better, though, he sat his own plastic dish besides hers and joined her for lunch.

He told her stories about the restaurant patrons, then stories of companies he'd rescued from the jaws of destruction, then stories again from their days in high school. Though Grace savored every word that came from his mouth, she also recognized that, in a limited way, he could talk about himself, about his company and about his work. He could talk about their distant past. He could even talk about the present. But he couldn't talk about the near past. He completely avoided any conversation about their life together now.

Struggling with tears, she set her fork beside her plate. A person didn't have to be a genius to figure out what was going on here. All you had to do was add the fact that she had to coax him into kissing her with the fact that he couldn't talk about the immediate past, and the fact that the things he told her about himself weren't too personal, and you came up with the obvious, painful truth.

He might have loved her at one time, but he didn't love her anymore, and he was planning to divorce her…

That is, if they weren't already divorced.

She looked down at her bare ring finger, noticed there wasn't even a tan line marking where a ring had been and admitted the ugly, painful truth to herself.

She and her husband were not together.

Chapter Five

"**Y**ou never were a big eater," Nick said, clearing away the remnants of her lunch as he prepared the area for them to play cards again.

"I guess not," Grace absently agreed, though she knew the truth was she'd lost her appetite when she realized the obvious. She and Nick must be separated, or in the throes of a divorce. That's why he was so standoffish. That's why she had to ask him to kiss her and why the kiss he gave her was so difficult for him. There was no other explanation that made any sense.

As quickly as she came to that conclusion, Grace realized something else equally obvious. From his behavior over the past few days, the way he'd cared for her and seen to her every want and whim, it was easy to see he couldn't possibly be at fault. A man who was good enough to stand by her when he didn't have to, a man who brought her clothes and perfume and sweetly bought her lunch from the restaurant across the street, wasn't a man who drove a woman to leave him. It had to be the other way around. She had probably driven Nick away.

So, now, not only was she facing the reality that she had no memory, and that her husband was planning to divorce her, she was also facing the bitter realization that something *she* had done had forced Nick away. She had lost her wonderful, brilliant, breathtakingly handsome husband because she was either foolish or shrewish.

Neither prospect was very heartening to a woman who couldn't remember her past. Both discouraged her from even *wanting* to get her memory back. Either dissuaded her from trying to envision the future.

They played cards until about seven-thirty, then Nick quietly reached for his jacket again. As before, he was animated and even happy with her until it was time to leave, then his mood shifted dramatically. Grace now understood that he got antsy and edgy because he didn't want to kiss her goodbye, but he knew that if he didn't, he would raise her suspicions.

And he wasn't supposed to say or do anything to upset her. Though she was drifting off to sleep at the time, she'd heard the doctor tell him that the night she was admitted.

Breathless, afraid he wouldn't kiss her and almost more afraid that he would, Grace sat poised, waiting. Nick slid into his soft leather jacket, adjusted the sleeves, checked the pockets, fixed the collar, then self-consciously walked to her bedside.

Grace's heart pounded in her chest. She met his eyes as he bent down, and the naked desire she read in their dark depths scrambled her pulse, even as it completely confused her. His eyes told her how very much he wanted to kiss her, negating everything she'd read in his actions only a few seconds before.

When his mouth grazed hers, the kiss, though chaste, was painfully poignant. Soft and reverent, his lips brushed over hers gently, until something sparked inside him, or maybe until he decided to set aside the past, and he deepened the kiss, but slowly and tenderly. The pure emotion of the kiss linked the hesitancy of his actions with the desire in his eyes. In a conclusion that was part analysis of actual events, and part instinct that felt very much like a memory—like a piece of her past trying to chip through the fog of her clouded thoughts—Grace realized that their marriage might be in trouble, but Nick still had feelings for her, feelings greater than duty or obligation. That was why it was so difficult for him to kiss her. He'd probably already said his final goodbye to her, and, if he still cared for her, with each kiss he was saying goodbye to her over and over again, ripping open tender wounds, testing the strength of the conviction he'd made when he'd decided to leave her.

Nick pulled away, and, without a word, walked to the door. He opened it and made a move as if he was about to go into the hall, but before he did, he turned to face her again. The look he gave her was so touchingly sad that Grace felt her heart break for him as much as it broke for herself.

Then he turned away once more and walked through the opening. The door swished softly closed behind him and Grace genuinely wondered if she'd ever see him again.

Frustrated, she pounded her pillow. What the hell could she have done to him to hurt him so much?

When Nick returned the next day, Grace watched him closely. He came with gifts: a new nightgown, new slippers and some body lotion in the same scent as the perfume he'd given her the day before. She thanked him, recognizing he'd brought the gifts to lift her spirits. Though he didn't know the exact depth of her thoughts, he knew that she hadn't misinterpreted the sadness in his expression when he'd left her the night before, and, generous person that he was, he was trying to make it up to her.

"Thank you," she said, swallowing the lump in her throat.

"You're welcome," he said, but as he spoke, the door to the room opened and Dr. Ringer entered.

"Good morning," he greeted exuberantly.

"Good morning," Nick returned uneasily, plumping her pillows as if doing something normal could somehow make everything okay again.

"How's the patient this morning?"

"She's great," Nick answered before Grace got the chance.

Dr. Ringer laughed. "Let me be the judge of that."

He gave Grace a quick examination and asked her some questions before taking a seat on the edge of the bed. "And you remember nothing?" he asked cautiously.

Tamping down the temptation to admit that she'd gotten a painful flash of insight the night before, Grace shook her head. She hadn't really had a memory. She'd merely realized that her husband might still have strong feelings for her, but he didn't want her anymore.

Trying to lighten the mood, she said, "Not unless you count the fact that I remembered I don't like carrots."

"I'd count it," Dr. Ringer said. "But I'd be much happier if you remembered something more tangible, like your occupation."

"Nick says I'm an accountant."

"That doesn't count."

"So what's the verdict?" Nick asked quietly, obviously concerned.

Dr. Ringer thought for a second. "Theoretically, I could send her home. Her vitals are fine...great. Her test results say there's nothing wrong. She's probably healthier than I am. But I'm a little concerned that after three days, she still doesn't have a clue who she is."

"*You're* concerned?" Grace asked with a laugh. "You should be me."

"You're troubled about your memory not returning yet?" the doctor asked.

"Not troubled," Grace said. "Not even really *concerned*. More like nervous."

"That's understandable," Dr. Ringer said.

"So, what are we going to do?" Nick asked and Grace gave him a sharp look. He seemed so anxious to hear the prognosis, Grace got the uncomfortable impression that he was trying to get rid of her. It was the first time since her accident that she felt he didn't want to be around her. He might not have wanted to kiss her, but he'd never seemed to mind being with her until today.

"I don't want to let her leave the hospital yet," Dr. Ringer announced slowly. Turning his attention to Grace, he said, "To be frank, you're the first concussion patient I've had who hasn't regained her memory within twenty-four hours. I'm not sure I trust letting you go home yet. I'd like the chance to do a little research before I release you." He paused, then, "How do you feel about staying a few more days?"

Grace licked her dry lips. Part of her desperately wanted to go home. She wanted real food. She wanted her own bed and bathroom, though she wasn't sure how she'd recognize them when she saw them. But another part of her knew, with absolute certainty, that Nick wouldn't be with her when she went home. She wasn't sure how he'd leave her—alone, without a memory—to fend for herself. But she knew he wouldn't be with her. And she couldn't stand the thought of losing him just yet.

"I think I'm better off here," she said softly, refusing to look at Nick.

Dr. Ringer patted her hand. "For the time being, I think you are, too."

The room was completely silent for a full minute after the doctor left. Through the entire time, Grace wouldn't look at Nick. Finally, when she couldn't stand the silence anymore, she glanced over at him and, to her surprise, he appeared relieved. Instead of that easing her own tension, the way he was acting unexpectedly compounded it. Made her believe he didn't so much mind being with her as much as he didn't want to take her to his home. Probably because he didn't want to have to pretend to share a house with her. Or maybe he didn't want to face telling her they weren't living together.

"So, cards again?" he said.

Grace smiled. In spite of the obvious problems in their relationship, he stood by her, played stupid cards twelve hours a day for the past two days, brought her food from the restaurant and answered the same questions over and over and over again because she frequently forgot what she'd asked.

"Is there anything else you'd prefer to do?"

"Actually, Grace, I like cards."

She nodded congenially. "Then cards it is. Besides rummy, what else do I know how to play?"

He took his seat beside her bed table, picked up the cards and began to shuffle. "You play hearts, pinochle, and you play poker." He paused, slanted her a carefree, happy smile. "Your brothers taught you."

The look he gave her nearly stole her breath. Not only did it make him appear young and even more handsome, but it was a loving, tender expression. It was a look you couldn't fake or conjure. It was a look that had to come from the heart. She tried not to make too much of it, even though she felt her own heart swell with nameless hope. He loved her. She *knew* he loved her. And somewhere down deep inside her, the belief began to form that if she could steal enough time with him, she could make him forget whatever had split them up, and get him to give her another chance.

But she knew that wasn't going to happen, because Dr. Ringer had only prolonged her visit for some research. In another few days he'd release her, and once she was released, she and Nick would go their separate ways.

She cleared her throat and put her thoughts back where they belonged. "I thought you said I only had one brother."

"Yes, but Angus raised Ryan Kelly at the same time that he took in you and Cal. So, because Ryan and Cal were nearly raised like twins, you thought of Ryan as a brother, too."

"Oh," she said, embarrassed. "You told me that, didn't you?"

"Yes," he said, then skimmed his fingertip down her nose. "But that's all part of the deal here," he said, and began to pass out the cards. "I don't mind repeating myself."

He gave her the look again. The gentle smile and the soft eyes that held the spark of the banked embers of desire for her. She could win him back. She *knew* she could. If only she had enough time to show him that she was different now. That she not only didn't know what she'd done, but if she knew what she'd done, she'd probably regret it more than any other mistake she'd made. Because whatever she'd done, it had to have been a mistake. No woman in her right mind would throw this man away.

They played cards until nearly eight o'clock. With only breaks for lunch and dinner, both of which Nick bought from the restaurant across the street, Grace and Nick passed the hours focusing their attention on games of chance, while their real-life game of chance went ignored. Instead, they laughed, teased, and absolutely avoided anything remotely like reality.

This time, at ten-to-eight when Nick rose to get his jacket, he wasn't as nervous as he had been the two nights before. He didn't fiddle with his sleeves, adjust his collar or even check his pockets for his keys. He slid the coat on with easy confidence, walked to her bedside, brushed her lips with a long, lingering kiss and smiled at her before leaving the room.

Steeped in contentment and joy, Grace settled against her pillow. As long as she could keep Dr. Ringer from releasing her too soon, she would be able to convince Nick it was okay to love her again. They had a spark so strong and so wonderful that if he could forget the past and concentrate on the future, their lives would be pure heaven.

Unfortunately, that also meant that if she wanted to keep Nick, she could never, ever regain her memories.

"Good morning."

Nick glanced over at the nurses' station to see Dr. Ringer leaning against the counter. From the way he straightened as Nick approached, Nick could tell the doctor had been waiting for him. "Hello, Dr. Ringer."

"I wanted to see you privately before I went in to see Grace this morning."

His words were so serious, so ominous, Nick's heart felt as if it had come to a crashing halt. "Why?"

The doctor motioned for Nick to join him in the small room off the nurses' station. He waited until they were seated at a round table before he said, "Frankly, I believe Grace is ready to go home, but I asked her to stay and laid the groundwork for her to stay even longer because I had an uncomfortable feeling yesterday that you didn't want to take her home."

Nick smiled casually. "She's not ready to go home."

"She's *afraid* to go home," Dr. Ringer countered. "I could see it in her eyes." He paused and skewered Nick with a shrewd, assessing stare. "Does she have reason to be afraid to go home, Mr. Spinelli?"

Insulted, Nick glared at the older man. "No, she does

not have reason to be afraid to go home. We don't fight and I don't hit her," he said, still looking the doctor in the eye. "If that's what you're implying."

"That wasn't what I was implying," the doctor said. "But if Grace has nothing to be afraid of, then I think she should be released today. From the research I've done, it's clear that if she hasn't regained her memory by now, she's not going to get it back until she's around familiar things. The quicker she's out of here, the quicker she's going to get her memory back."

Nick shook his head. Not only did he not want to take Grace to his home with its spare, very masculine bedroom, but he knew bringing her there wouldn't accomplish Dr. Ringer's purposes anyway. She wouldn't remember anything because she wouldn't encounter anything familiar.

"That's up to Grace," Nick said. "I don't want to take her home before she feels she's ready."

"Mr. Spinelli, your wife is fine, and insurance isn't going to allow her to stay much longer."

"Dr. Ringer," Nick said, smiling thinly, "I'm a millionaire several times over. Grace's father is a billionaire. If the insurance company doesn't want to pay for any additional time Grace feels she needs here, then I'll happily pick up the tab."

Chuckling self-consciously, Dr. Ringer said, "You're getting the wrong impression. I'm not as concerned about your insurance as I am concerned about Grace. I genuinely believe it's time for Grace to go home."

"And I think you're wrong. You say you saw fear in her eyes yesterday. Did you ever stop to think that might be because she's afraid to be too far away from a medical professional?"

Dr. Ringer thought for a minute. "It could be."

"That's how I'm interpreting it. She has nothing else to be afraid of." At least, Nick didn't think so. Given that he had no idea what her real life was like, Nick didn't really know. The fact that Dr. Ringer believed she was afraid of something reinforced Nick's decision that he wouldn't release her into anyone's care but Angus's. But it also brought another, stronger, more emotional reaction. If she had a boyfriend or lover who abused her, so help him, Nick knew he'd kill him.

"Then you won't mind if I see Grace alone this morning?" the doctor said.

"No, certainly not," Nick said, then rose and began walking out of the room. "I'll go for doughnuts. I'll be back in twenty minutes."

But Nick got only as far as the door before raw emotion compelled him to turn around and face the doctor again. "Dr. Ringer, I love my wife," Nick said and realized it was true. Even after ten years and all the conflicts that still existed between them, he loved her. He adored her. He almost didn't know how he'd live without her when the time came for him to let her go again. But he also knew he had to let her go again. The reasons were obvious to him. First, he had no idea what her life was like. He didn't know if she had a boyfriend or lover, or even a fiancé. A fiancé seemed like a logical reason for her to have come to see him—seeking a divorce, if the marriage certificate on her front seat was any indicator. The mere thought blinded him with pain, but Nick ignored it because there was a second reason he knew he'd have to brace himself to live without her. This one was more important than the first.

Once she got her memory back, she wouldn't want him anymore. He'd hurt her in the worst possible way, and, once she remembered that, anger and pain wouldn't be too far behind. He only hoped his leaving her hadn't damaged her self-worth so much that she might have gotten involved with a man who was abusing her.

"I love Grace more than anything in the world," Nick

said, still holding the doctor's gaze. "I wouldn't do anything to hurt her. *Anything.*"

And God help the person who did, Nick thought and pushed himself through the nurses' station, down the hall and out of the building, desperately in need of some cool morning air.

Grace glanced up from her hospital menu and saw Dr. Ringer. "Hi," she said, surprised he was here so early. "I didn't expect to see you yet."

"I wanted to beat your husband in this morning."

Though his words were light and friendly, Grace's heart skipped a beat. "Why?"

Dr. Ringer sat on the chair by the bed—Nick's chair. "Well, you are the patient, but he appears to be doing a lot of talking for you."

Grace smiled. "He can be a bit authoritative."

"That's putting it mildly. But we're not here to talk about Nick. We're here to talk about you. And since he's not here, I want the *real* scoop."

Grace drew a long breath. "The real scoop is that I haven't had an actual memory."

The doctor speared her with a hard look. "I caught that, Grace. Don't stop now. If you didn't have an actual memory, what did you have?"

Grace sighed heavily. Part of her didn't want to admit this, the other part knew it wasn't fair to withhold this kind of information from the man who was trying to cure her. "A feeling. More than intuition." She stopped, collected her thoughts. "I just suddenly *knew* something."

"What was that?"

Thinking she'd done her part by disclosing what she had, and not willing to reveal more, Grace cleared her throat. "Well, truthfully, I'd rather not talk about it."

Dr. Ringer leaned back in his chair. "Grace, you know you can tell me anything."

She nodded. "I know, but because this is more of a feeling than fact, I'd rather not say right now."

"Just answer me this, then. Yesterday, I got the impression you were afraid to go home. Does that have anything to do with this feeling? Are you *afraid* of your husband?"

Grace smiled with relief. "Oh, heavens, no. He's the most wonderful man on the face of the earth."

"So, you'd be very comfortable going home with him?"

"Yes." What she was afraid of was that he didn't want to take her home or *couldn't* take her to his home because they were separated. That's what she couldn't tell Dr. Ringer.

"Then, I think you should go home."

"I *can't* go home."

The doctor stared at her. "Okay, you're not afraid of your husband, but you *can't* go home and he's not too keen about taking you home. So, what am I supposed to do? What am I supposed to *think?*"

"I didn't mean to say *can't*," Grace quickly corrected. "What I wanted to say was that I don't want to be out of the hospital yet. If I can't remember, I must still need care."

He shook his head. "Grace, some people never regain their memory."

"I know that."

"Is *that* what you're afraid of?"

The very thought made her laugh. "Actually, I think I'm more afraid of what I'll find when I do get my memory back."

Again, Dr. Ringer gave her an astute look. "Grace, you do realize your fear of remembering could be what's holding you back?"

"No. I never thought of that."

"It's a common belief that people who have problems

in their lives sometimes don't regain their memory because they don't *want* to go back to all their problems.''

Though the doctor didn't understand the implications of what he'd just told her, Grace went perfectly still. If her marriage really was falling apart, particularly if she was responsible for her marriage falling apart, it seemed highly possible that she could be keeping her memories away. She closed her eyes and leaned back on her pillow.

''Grace, I've spoken with Nick and he tells me that not only are the two of you financially solvent, but you must get along very well because he said you don't fight.''

Of course they don't. They were probably already separated.

''I think it's time to leave today. Nick loves you. He'll take good care of you. And it sounds like you have a wonderful life to go back to.''

She didn't. She knew she didn't. Dr. Ringer was only seeing the side of the story related by Nick. But she knew otherwise. She had a gut-level feeling, backed up by Nick's continued hesitancy and resistance, that in spite of the fact that they loved each other, their marriage had fallen apart.

To the doctor she said, ''Why don't we give it another day or two? I'm not ready to upset the applecart yet.''

''Grace, wouldn't it be better to know the truth about this than to live a lie?''

She smiled ruefully. ''We don't really know I'm living a lie.''

''Okay, fine. You're right. We don't really know anything about your life, except what Nick tells us. But what bothers me is that you don't *want* to get the answers.''

''That's not true. I just want to be sure I get to the answers the right way and at the right time.''

''All right, then, how about this? I have a psychiatrist friend who sometimes travels to Turner when I need her. I could have Christine come down and talk with you.''

He paused for a moment. "Your whole problem might be nothing more than a refusal to remember because you're afraid of what you'll find once you do remember," he said finally. "For all we know, your continued memory loss might be the result of being afraid to drive after your accident. It could even be that you're afraid to remember because you don't know what you'll find. If you talked with Christine and she alleviated your fears, you might discover the only thing you're afraid of is *not* knowing."

Grace didn't want to see his psychiatrist friend, but Dr. Ringer was right about one thing. She was afraid to remember because she *didn't* know what she'd find. All she had was a gut instinct, but that instinct was so strong and so pure, it would be enough to frighten anyone into refusing to probe for the past.

Grace drew a quiet breath. What could she have done that was so bad that she'd rather live in darkness than remember?

When Grace didn't answer him, Dr. Ringer started to leave. "Grace, you have to go home sometime," he said, pushing her up against the wall of unrelenting truth. She did have to go home sometime.

"Though your husband tells me that he and your father can afford to pay for indefinite care, this isn't that kind of facility."

Fear washed over her but Grace nodded unemotionally. Without realizing it, the doctor had just clued her in to two important things. First, one way or another he was getting her out of this hospital and into the world of her memories, if only to force her back into her real life. Second, he and Nick had talked about indefinite care, which confirmed at least part of what she instinctively knew— Nick really didn't want to take her home.

"In order to handle my practice fairly," Dr. Ringer said, "I have to report to your insurance company that I believe you're ready to be released."

Grace nodded. Her plans were ruined, snuffed out in a quick puff of smoke. He was going to release her before she had a chance to convince Nick it was okay to love her again. And if she didn't have time to convince Nick it was okay to love her again, this time tomorrow night she'd be alone. Alone. No memories meant there was not one other soul on the face of the earth she knew, or at least remembered. She would be a stranger in her own family. But, most of all, leaving the hospital meant no Nick. No patient eyes, no loving smiles, no stolen kisses.

As she reluctantly nodded her understanding, Nick pushed open her door. He held two plastic cups of coffee and a bulging bag bearing the logo of a doughnut shop. "Hey, what's this?" he asked, teasing. "Having a consultation without me?"

Dr. Ringer glanced at Grace and she froze. Somehow, someway, she had to force Nick's hand. She had to get him into a position where he had no choice but to take her home, because if she gave him a choice, it was over. She wouldn't get the chance to win him back.

Chapter Six

Grace's expression stopped Nick cold. Her already pale skin was colorless. She didn't take her eyes off the door for several seconds after the doctor walked out of the room. Her fingers were knitted together and she was squeezing so hard her knuckles had whitened. He knew Dr. Ringer wouldn't force her out of the hospital before she was ready. Nick had seen to that part of the problem in his own discussion with the man. So, something else was troubling her.

"I brought you doughnuts," he offered carefully.

As if breaking out of a trace, she shook her head and looked at him. "What?"

"I brought you doughnuts."

"What kind?" she asked excitedly, back to her old self again.

"Well, I got chocolate glazed...your favorite. But I also brought blueberry cake and strawberry-cream filled since I wasn't exactly sure what mood you'd be in this morning."

And he still didn't know. She might be feigning cheerfulness, but something had happened. If Nick were a betting man, he'd think she'd remembered something.

"I'll take the blueberry."

"See. I'm glad I got extras. You didn't go for your favorite. You took your usual second choice."

"Maybe the concussion made me different," Grace suggested casually, but her tone alerted Nick that for her this was a serious topic.

"Do you think I'm different?"

"Yes," Nick said with a quick laugh, trying to lighten the mood and glad he could do it without lying, because the truth was, she was different, very different to him. "I definitely think you're different."

"In what way?"

"Well, you chose your second-favorite doughnut," he said, still flippant. He wasn't ready for her to get serious yet. For the past few days he'd avoided her questions, evaded her questions and made light of her questions. He had no reason to believe that strategy wouldn't work now.

"That's not an important difference. Doughnuts are inconsequential. I want something with substance."

Since he couldn't give her substance, he busied himself distributing the doughnuts and hedged the truth again by glibly saying, "Substance is in the eye of the beholder. A doughnut choice usually is a big deal to you."

She studied him for a minute. "Well, then, can you at least tell me this? Are the changes for the better? If I'm different, am I different in a better way?"

"Yes," he replied unequivocally because he not only didn't see the harm in that, but for him, after ten years, it was the absolute truth.

His answer appeared to please her and, comfortable that she was satisfied enough to drop the subject, Nick slipped out of his jacket and removed the lid from his coffee. "So, what'll it be this morning? Rummy, hearts, pinochle?"

She didn't say anything for several seconds, waiting, it

seemed, to catch his gaze. When she did, Nick saw that her violet eyes nearly glowed with challenge. "I want to play poker."

"Oh, do you now?" Nick asked, chuckling. "And what, exactly, would the stakes of this game be?"

"If you win," she said, still holding his gaze, "you name your prize. Whatever you want from me, you ask and it's yours."

Something about the way she said that caused a knot to form in Nick's stomach. He knew she hadn't remembered any of her past or she'd be demanding answers right now, but that didn't mean her intuition was off—or maybe his evading wasn't as good as he'd thought. She was offering him the opportunity to have whatever he wanted. For all she knew, Nick could demand anything from a long, steamy night of sex to the opportunity to walk out the door and not come back. Gazing into her eyes, he knew she understood what she was risking. The only thing he couldn't figure out was what had happened to cause her to risk it.

Striving to be casual, he plucked the deck of cards from the top drawer of her beside table. He began to shuffle. "And if you win?"

Again, she didn't say anything until he looked at her. With the rhythmic shuffling of the cards in the background, she waited until the light in her violet eyes nearly had him hypnotized before she said, "You take me home tomorrow."

"What if Dr. Ringer won't release you tomorrow?"

"We both know Dr. Ringer wants me to leave today." He shuffled some more. "Yes, he told me."

"So, are you going to deal?"

"Aren't you even interested in what I'll ask for if I win?"

"You're not going to win."

"That's right, because I'm not going to play."

"Are you chicken?" she asked softly.

This time he caught her gaze. "No."

"Then you shouldn't have anything to worry about."

"I'm not taking you home until I think you're ready, and I don't think you're ready," Nick said, but sweat began to bead on his neck. It didn't bother him so much that she wanted to go home, what bothered him was that she knew he didn't want to take her. That's what caused her willingness to risk offering him his choice of reward if he won. She already knew what he would ask for.

"Well, I think I am ready," Grace countered and Nick bit back a curse.

They both knew that if Grace wanted to leave the hospital badly enough, she could. Dr. Ringer was ready to release her if only in the hope of stimulating her memory. All she had to do was tell the doctor she felt she'd get her memory back more readily in familiar surroundings and he'd let her go without a moment's hesitation, and, unless Nick wanted to explain the uncomfortable truth, he would be *forced* to take her home.

But Grace had figured out that he didn't want to do that, and, using the uniquely MacFarland perception of fair play, she was giving him an even chance. If he really wanted her to stay in the hospital, all he had to do was beat her at cards. In a sense, their next move would be decided by fate.

He shuffled again. "Five-card stud. Two-card draw. Nothing wild. Best hand wins. And this isn't a one-hand game. We're going for best two out of three." At least this way he upped his odds. Making it more than one game precluded her beating him by sheer luck, plus, if she hadn't played in a while, it would take her more than three hands to recall her strategies. Now all he had to do was hope that she didn't inadvertently get two lucky hands before he skillfully beat her at three.

He dealt the cards. She drew her two, but Nick stood

pat. "I have a straight," he said, grinning as he showed his cards.

"Pure luck," she said and took the cards herself this time. "I'll deal this one."

If he wouldn't have known Grace to be honest and trustworthy, he would have wondered about her full house. However, he did know her to be honest. Unfortunately, that didn't change the fact that they were now tied at one hand each.

"You want to deal again?" he asked, catching her gaze.

Nervous, she shook her head. If nothing else, her refusal to deal proved she hadn't cheated. He picked up the deck and shuffled several times before he handed out the cards. He drew two tens, a king, a queen and an ace. Realizing two tens could win this game, he kept them, as well as the ace for a high card.

Chewing her bottom lip, Grace motioned for two cards. Without picking up the deck, he dealt her two from the top, then said a silent prayer that she would lose. He didn't want to take her home.

He *couldn't* take her home. Not only would she not regain her memory looking at things she'd never seen before, but he was growing attached to her. He was reading her moods, able to gauge her feelings. He didn't like to see her hurt, and couldn't stand the thought that someone or something in her life filled her with fear.

He couldn't stop thinking that she probably had a fiancé and that's why she had been on her way to Turner—to get a divorce. So, it wouldn't be proper or prudent to live with her until Angus got home. But even if he could find out the name of her possible fiancé, Nick wouldn't release Grace into the care of someone who might actually be the source of her fear. His only hope was to keep her in the hospital.

He drew in his first card. Another ace. Two pair.

Relaxing a little, he glanced at Grace. She stared at her cards as if trying to ascertain the best way to play them. A good sign. That meant she didn't have something as straightforward as three of a kind.

He drew in his second card. A six. No help. But no damage, either. After all, he had two pair.

"What do you have?"

She looked up at him. Her eyes were serious and solemn, as if this meant a great deal to her. He didn't care. She couldn't go home with him. She didn't understand that there were no memories for her there. She didn't know that what she needed was to go to Angus's ranch, where she had friends and family and memories galore. And he couldn't tell her without upsetting her and maybe even getting into an ugly confrontation, which might prevent the return of her memory for even longer.

"I'd rather you show your cards first."

Nick shook his head. "It's your turn."

"I know," she said, "but more is at stake here for me than for you."

"How do you know? You don't know what I'm going to ask for."

She caught his gaze again. "We both know that you're going to ask for the exact opposite of what I want," she said, holding his eyes prisoner.

"Only because I believe you have a much better chance of a complete recovery here at the hospital."

"Dr. Ringer said that there is nothing wrong with me."

"I know, but I just think it's safer here."

"For whom?"

He sighed, not wanting to get into that argument. "Show me your cards."

"You show me yours."

"All right," he said, setting his cards on her bed table. "Two pair. Tens and aces."

Her mouth fell open in surprise and Nick almost felt

guilty for taking advantage of her. "Sorry," he said and started to pick up the cards, but Grace stopped him.

"I have three twos," she said, sounding amazed. Then she grinned up at him. "Well, what do you know? It looks like I'm going home."

Nick glanced around his bedroom and wondered what else he'd have to do to make it look like a woman also slept here. He'd already traded his geometric-print bedspread and curtains for something frilly and floral, both of which were purchased by his housekeeper. Stella had also gone to the drugstore for him and bought duplicates of the makeup and skin-care products he'd found in her suitcase, as well as other makeup that would complement the things he'd found but that Grace didn't have and would probably need.

Then Nick himself had gone to a secondhand store to fill the closet with women's clothes in Grace's size. He'd purchased a few things new, the more personal things like undergarments and nightclothes. Stella had run them through the washer twice to help them lose the "unworn" feeling, but he also recognized that if he only put new things in her closet and drawers, nothing would be dated. He wanted her to be comfortable and happy until Angus and Cal returned from Houston next week. But more than that, he didn't want her to have new questions. The old questions were difficult enough for both of them, particularly considering the card game.

When he discovered Dr. Ringer had been trying to talk her into leaving, Nick wondered if the deck hadn't been stacked against him all along. But he also realized it hadn't necessarily been her intention to *win* that card game. From the way she'd set things up, she might have actually wanted to lose in order to give Nick the opportunity to tell her that what he wanted most in the world was for her *not* to come home with him, if only because it would get their uncomfortable truth out in the open.

Well, even if he'd lost, he couldn't do that. Even though bringing her home was a great inconvenience, even though bringing her home forced him into his housekeeper's confidence about their marriage and Grace's amnesia, changed his life and brought him face-to-face with the prospect of being alone with her in a beautiful, romantic mountain retreat for over a week, he wasn't about to tell her she couldn't come home with him. If he did, he'd have to explain their past. He'd have to tell her about his father. He'd have to admit the way he'd lived all those years. But, more than that, he'd have to endure her justified anger for saying goodbye with a note instead of having the courage to talk with her.

And he'd have to keep her for the entire week anyway, because there was still no one home at the MacFarland ranch, and he wasn't leaving her with a fiancé or boyfriend he didn't trust. The only good thing about this deal was that Grace was so excited about her discharge the next morning, she hadn't minded Nick leaving early.

So now here he stood, ten minutes before it was time to pick her up and bring her home, as nervous as he'd been on their wedding night...

The analogy didn't soothe him.

That morning, Grace's pre-Nick visitor was a woman, not Dr. Ringer. But Grace had been expecting her. "You must be Christine," she said as the tall blonde entered the room.

"Christine Warner. How did you know?"

"Dr. Ringer mentioned that he wanted me to speak with you. Since I'm leaving today, I figured he'd send his psychiatrist friend down to break the ice, because he'll probably want us to start seeing each other regularly."

"I'm not here to drum up business," the woman said.

"He told me about your conversation yesterday morning, and *that's* why I'm here."

"We talked about a lot of things yesterday morning."

"Well," Christine said, walking to the foot of Grace's bed, "specifically, he told me about the part where he thinks you're not getting your memory back because you're afraid of what you'll remember."

"That's probably true," Grace admitted softly.

Christine conceded that point with a nod. "He also told me that yesterday morning you didn't want to go home. Why the sudden change of heart?"

There was no way Grace would ever tell this woman the truth, but that didn't mean she had to lie, either. "I guess I realized that going home I'd be able to spend more time with my husband."

"I understand he's here every day."

"Yes, but I want to see him as he really is," Grace told her. "He's been good, sweet, patient and kind here, but all that might change once we get out of the hospital. I want to know if I really love him, or if I only love a man who's been very good to me because I was sick."

Christine thought about that for a second, then she laughed. "You know, in a roundabout way, I see your point. What are you going to do if you see him as he really is and you decide you don't love him?"

"I have a father and a brother...and an adoptive brother. He's told me their names. He's told me where they live. If things don't turn out okay, I'll contact them."

"You wouldn't feel like calling them now, would you?"

"I did try to call them, but they're in Houston...just like Nick told me they were," Grace said, confirming for Christine that she'd checked up on Nick and he hadn't been lying to her.

Christine nodded her acceptance of that. "Will you do me a favor?"

"What?"

"Will you make an appointment to see me next week, say, Tuesday?"

Realizing she did need some guidance through this, and that Christine had been neither judgmental nor negative about Grace's decision, only open-minded, Grace decided that seeing her once a week would be a wonderful idea.

"Yeah. I'll be in next Tuesday. I'll be in every Tuesday until I get my memory back if you think that will do any good."

"Well, it might not do a whole heck of a lot of good," Christine said, walking to the door. "But," she added, winking at Grace, "it might not hurt to have a friend, either."

Grace couldn't have agreed more.

Chapter Seven

"So, this is the house you were bragging about?" Grace said as they pulled up beside what looked to be a three-story log cabin. Nestled in a thick forest enhanced by the yellow, orange and copper leaves of autumn, the house was a huge, elaborate menagerie of angles and windows. It was so beautiful it stole her breath—the same way looking at the man beside her frequently did.

She only teased Nick about the house because she felt he needed teasing. He'd been quiet and sullen the entire drive, and she knew this wasn't easy for him. He probably felt that being with her in this house might bring back painful memories for him, but if it did, it would eventually bring back painful memories for her, too.

Grace only hoped she wasn't slapped with reality the minute she stepped over the threshold. She needed enough time alone with Nick that she could convince him to put their negative past behind them.

"Yes. This is the house I've been bragging about," Nick said, pretending to be cheerful as he pushed open the door of his shiny black Jimmy. If she had any doubts about how much money he had, first his vehicle, then the house would have eased them. She knew unequivocally that he wasn't being nice to her to get to her father's fortune, and though that hadn't come up as a consideration before, it was nice to know it wouldn't have to enter the picture at all.

He came around the hood of the car and opened the door for her. When Nick took her hand to help her out, a current of electricity coursed up her arm. Her gaze automatically swung to Nick, who patently ignored the reaction, but Grace could see he was biting his bottom lip.

Yes, there was something here. Something vital. Something strong. Something *important*. And she'd be damned if she was letting it go without a fight.

"Thanks," she said when she was on the ground and able to make her way to the stone sidewalk.

"You're welcome," Nick said, opening the back door of the truck to get her suitcase.

Grace had to admit that when she saw the small paisley bag he'd brought to pack her meager belongings, she recognized it. She'd fully, completely and actually recognized it, and knew it was hers. Unfortunately, the little town of Turner, Nick's truck, the road to their home, even the house itself hadn't stirred one familiar thought. It was irritating and frustrating that a suitcase and some carrots came in as clear as a bell, but the things most important to her—her husband, her home and her hometown— hadn't registered at all.

She waited until Nick met her on the walkway and grasped her elbow before starting up to the porch. Feeling very much like an interloper, she let him open the front door.

She closed her eyes and took a deep, long breath for courage, then raised her eyelids and entered the foyer of her home.

A combination of regret and relief swamped her as she

glanced around the unexpectedly formal entryway. Despite the fact that the house was made of logs, the foyer walls were plastered, Oriental rugs accented the white ceramic-tile floor and a simple but elegant chandelier hung from the cathedral ceiling.

"It's beautiful," she gasped, gazing around as regret over her still-lost memory warred with relief that she didn't yet have to face her past and might even have time to correct it.

"But it didn't help you remember anything," Nick speculated, watching her.

She hung her head. "No, I'm sorry, Nick. It didn't."

"Grace, please," Nick implored, setting her suitcase on the floor so he could hold her shoulders to comfort her. "Don't worry about me. And don't worry about your memory. There's plenty of time to—"

"So, this is Grace."

Nick's soothing had been interrupted by a strong, nasal voice. With the spell of the moment broken, curiosity overrode the need for comfort, and Grace peeked behind her to see a short, middle-aged woman standing in front of the entry to the formal dining room. Her dyed blond hair was cut short and her ample bosom strained against the buttons of her butterscotch housekeeper's uniform.

"Yes, this is Grace," Nick replied and Grace noted the tone of exasperated humor in his voice. "Grace, this is my...*our* housekeeper, Stella."

Grace hadn't missed that slip. She also hadn't missed the fact that the housekeeper didn't know her, or the way the woman seemed overly interested to finally meet her. Deciding to ignore all that because it only pointed to a conclusion she'd already made—she and Nick were separated—Grace extended her hand as if she was making a new acquaintance, which she probably was, given Stella's reaction to her. "Hi."

"Hi, yourself," Stella said. "So, how are you doing?"

"Stella's from the Bronx," Nick explained, picking up Grace's suitcase again. "Her son got a job in Turner and moved her grandchildren down here, and she followed them."

"It was mean and spiteful to insinuate myself on them this way," Stella acknowledged merrily, batting a hand. "I got a job to keep myself occupied so I don't spend every waking minute at their house. They deserve some peace. Just not so much that I never get to see my grandchildren."

Grace couldn't help herself, she laughed. Something about Stella's slightly overbearing attitude appealed to her. "I'm sure your grandchildren love the attention."

"Yeah, but their parents have bouts of wanting to shoot me."

Again, the housekeeper's attitude made her laugh. If it wasn't for the fact that Stella obviously hadn't met Grace before, Grace would think she knew her...or someone like her. That was it. She must know someone very much like her.

Walking up the stairs, she questioned Nick about it. "I could tell this was the first time I met Stella," Grace said. "But I know someone like her, don't I?"

Before he replied, Nick berated himself for the stupid mistake. He should have warned Stella to pretend she knew Grace. Since Grace wasn't questioning why she didn't know Stella, Nick chose not to answer that question until he had to. Instead, he considered that Stella actually was very much like Grace's father, Angus, and decided it couldn't hurt to tell Grace that. "Though Stella has that New York nasal tone and Angus still has something of a Scottish burr in his voice," he told her, "Stella and Angus could pass for family."

"They look alike?" Grace asked curiously, following Nick up a second flight of stairs.

He shook his head. "No, they talk alike. But it's not

how they talk, it's what they say. Without admitting that both are nosy, I'd suggest that both are fiercely protective of their families. They love their children to the point of being overly concerned.''

"I can't wait until my father gets back from Houston."

Hearing the note of sadness in her voice, Nick stopped walking. "I'm really sorry about that, Grace. I have no idea where they are in Houston. I've called hotels, and even offered money, but no one will tell me where they are. It would seem Angus has given the hotel desk clerks more money to keep his whereabouts a secret."

"You make him sound like a celebrity."

"No, he's more of a man who likes his privacy. And, because he's notorious for investing in some pretty wacky things, he's also a man who probably gets hounded to death by people who want to pitch their ideas." Turning to lead Grace to his room, Nick added, "But he'll be home soon. Only a little over a week."

One long, torturous week, Nick thought, then pushed open the door to his room, revealing a huge space now so elegantly appointed that Nick couldn't help liking it. He thought he might keep the decor if it wouldn't bring back too many memories of Grace after she was gone.

Grace confirmed his opinion. "Oh, Nick," she gasped. "It's wonderful."

Leaning against the doorjamb, Nick smiled. In his good, eighteen-year-old dreams, he'd imagined himself giving Grace a fabulous home like this. He'd also imagined her reaction to be very much like what it was now. He felt himself glow with pride, though he knew in another week all this would be over.

"Mauve, almond and wine," he said, spouting the color information he'd gotten from the sales tags of the curtains and bedspread. "They all mix well with your coloring. I think that's why we chose these."

He knew he'd deliberately misled her into believing she

was part of the "we" that had done the choosing, but he hadn't really lied. And besides, the statement had actually backfired. As soon as he realized how well the shades would match her complexion and hair color, he envisioned her naked, tangled in the covers. He saw her sable-hued hair fanned across the pillow. He saw moonlight spilling in through the panes of the French doors, accenting her creamy skin.

Gritting his teeth to suppress a surge of desire, he got his mind on other things, more pertinent things, by saying, "I think it might be a good idea if you took a few minutes to rest before we unpack your belongings."

"Don't be silly," Grace said, happily looking around the room, feeling that though she didn't recognize it, she adored it. Because the whole decorating scheme was something she would have chosen, she felt a swell of hope. She might be gone from Nick's life, but he'd kept her bedroom. "I'm perfectly fine. I'll unpack and then you can show me the rest of the house."

"You're sure you're not tired?"

She smiled. "Positive." Without waiting for Nick's approval, Grace snapped open the suitcase which he'd laid on the bed.

Nick tried to nudge her hands away. "I'll help you with this stuff."

"No, I want to see if I remember anything, if anything comes naturally."

Nick shook his head. "I don't think that's a good idea. Let's not push it."

"This isn't pushing it," Grace argued. "This is a little test, that's all."

Though Nick wasn't pleased, he didn't try to stop her, but watched carefully as she opened drawers attempting to locate the proper places to store the things she pulled from her bag.

Finally, after having familiarized herself with all the

drawers, she sighed heavily. Though it was her intention to push herself to the wall, to make absolutely sure that a memory wouldn't sneak up on her when she didn't want it to, Grace had tired herself out opening and closing every drawer in the room. "You were right. I shouldn't have done that."

"See, you should have rested."

She was tempted to ask him if that was part of the reason they were getting divorced. That she was stubborn, single-minded, and uncompromising. But she stopped herself. She'd passed the test of touching her most intimate, personal things and hadn't gotten one memory, so she knew she had some time to convince Nick to love her again. She also realized it wasn't wise to push any further, any faster than what she'd already pushed.

Still, one thing troubled her enough that she felt she should get it out in the open. "I didn't find any of your things while I was investigating every drawer in the room."

Without taking his eyes off her, Nick said, "Stella and I moved my things into one of the other bedrooms. You're sick, and in no condition to be jostled by another person in bed with you."

His answer was so reasonable that Grace couldn't argue. But it was also so pat that it could have been a convenient excuse. She decided again that it was too soon to push, and, slapping her hands on her thighs, rose from the bed. "Let's get that tour."

"I thought you said you were tired."

"I am, but I'll never increase my stamina if I don't overextend myself at least a little bit."

He shook his head. "Not today. Too much has happened already today. Tomorrow, you can overextend. Right now, I'm going to have Stella whip up something for us for lunch, then you're taking a nap."

She would have argued about the nap, except it seemed

as if he was planning to eat with her. One victory at a time, she told herself. There was no sense being greedy.

"Three aces."

Grace grinned. "Sorry, full house."

"Damned if she doesn't have the luck of the Irish," Stella said to Nick as she tossed her cards to the table in the sunroom.

"I told you," Nick said, laughing at Stella who prided herself on being "the best" at poker. "I could beat her at hearts. I could beat her at rummy. But there's no one better at poker than Grace."

And if he had remembered she was this good at poker, he would have demanded they play gin rummy the day she challenged him for her freedom. But all that was water under the bridge and things really hadn't gone too badly over the past two days. They played cards, read and took periodic walks through the woods surrounding the house. Her mood was better. *His* mood was better. Stella's mood had gone straight to hell because she'd lost fifteen dollars when she insisted she needed to play for money to get her juices flowing. But the bottom line was, Grace was obviously feeling better. And to Nick, right at this moment, that was all that counted.

"I think it's time for the patient to get a little fresh air and sunshine," Nick said, pulling Grace's chair away from the table.

"You can't take her now, I'm just starting to get lucky."

"You lost the last thirteen hands," Nick reminded Stella as he handed Grace a sweater.

"And thirteen's an unlucky number," Stella reasoned logically, though Nick could swear she was crazy. "Which means game fourteen has got to be my lucky game."

"If thirteen's such an unlucky number, why wasn't it unlucky for Grace?"

"I don't know," Stella said, and even to Nick it sounded as if she was pouting.

"Well, we'll figure it out tomorrow."

"Tomorrow?"

"Grace has had a busy day. Right now, we're going to take a walk. You're going to fix some dinner. And we're all going to call it an early night."

"Oh no you don't..."

"But, Nick..."

Grace and Stella protested simultaneously, and Nick held up a cautionary hand. "You don't get any say in the matter," he said to Stella, then he turned to Grace. "And you stayed up too late last night. Tonight, you're getting to bed on time."

"You sound like my father," Grace said, leading him to the sliding door of the ground-level sunroom.

His heart frozen with trepidation, Nick stopped Grace. "You remember your father?"

She considered that. "No. That comment just came out."

"Well, Grace, that might be a very good sign," Nick said, feeling guilty again because those kinds of flashes of insight were proof that in the right surroundings she probably would be remembering much, much more. But he couldn't let her go home. He just couldn't. Every day she got stronger, happier. And to Nick her lack of anxiety over the past couple of days was as much a sign that she had something to fear at home as her snatches of memory were a sign that she'd make a full recovery in the right surroundings. But even though he knew he'd done the right thing by bringing her to his house, Nick couldn't stop the surge of guilt. Or the sadness. Because when Angus returned and everything could be made right for Grace again, Nick would lose her.

Grace noticed the change immediately and she bit back a sigh. Most of the time, Nick was lighthearted and carefree, and behaved like a normal husband. In those times, they laughed and talked, played cards with Stella, ate Stella's wonderful meals and watched the fire in the ground-floor fireplace. At those times, Grace felt the bond rejuvenating, rebuilding, strengthening. And at those times, she genuinely believed it was only a matter of time before Nick would come to see that whatever had happened between them before was meaningless, and that the only thing that mattered was how they felt about each other now.

But there were other times, specifically when the conversation drifted to whether or not she was regaining her memory, when Nick would become sullen, or confused, or appear to be guilt-ridden, or even borderline angry.

She knew that nothing she had done had caused his mood. She also sensed that nothing from their past caused that mood, either. Rather, she felt his odd moods occurred whenever he realized their time together was ending, which he apparently believed would happen when her memory returned and she remembered the truth about their relationship.

"I sometimes have the feeling you don't want me to get my memory back." She hadn't meant to say that, but once it was out she was glad she had.

"I just want you to be all right."

She stopped walking. Sunlight filtered through the red, auburn and golden leaves of the trees shrouding Nick's property. A thick blanket of those same leaves lay at her feet. "And what exactly is *all right*? I'm healthy, I'm happy, I'm home. Could we not argue with success?"

Unexpectedly, Nick laughed. "You know, Grace, that's probably the smartest thing you've ever said to me and you've said some pretty smart things."

Glad that she'd broken the dreary spell, she took the

two steps that separated them and tugged on the ends of the collar of his jacket. "Like what?"

Instinctively, he wrapped his arms around her. Grace snuggled into his warmth.

"Well, you once told me that if I really hated our hometown, Crossroads Creek..." He gave her a look to see if that sparked any memory. She nodded once to indicate she heard, but it hadn't helped.

"You once told me that if I really hated our hometown," he continued, "I shouldn't run away. I should leave to go to college."

Grace frowned at him. "How is that so brilliant?" she said, sounding confused.

Nick drew a breath and expelled it in a long puff as he considered how to answer her. She didn't know anything about his home or his family life. She hadn't known about his home or his family while they were dating, either, but his persona was so different, so rebellious back then that she hadn't questioned why he wouldn't think of college first.

Deciding that it wouldn't hurt to explain he'd been poor, that his parents hadn't talked much about college or encouraged him to go, and that he himself hadn't had a clue of what he wanted to be, Nick said, "It was brilliant because my family was pretty poor and I never saw college as an escape route. I saw it as a luxury. You showed me a different perspective."

"That's good. Everybody should have their perspective jiggled every once in a while."

Nick laughed. "And how would you know? Your perspective was the last perspective that anybody could *jiggle*. In case you haven't noticed a pattern in my stories so far, you've been the one changing me. Not vice versa."

Grace couldn't help it, her breath caught. "Oh, Nick, I'm sorry. Was I that bad?"

For a few seconds, Nick only stared at her, seemingly

not understanding what she was driving at. When her meaning hit him, he gasped. "Oh, no. No, Grace. The only changes you ever made in me were good."

Then what went wrong? She almost asked it. But his arms had come around her so naturally. And he wasn't jittery or jumpy. They were so close their frosted breaths mingled in the early-autumn air. He hadn't held her in two days. The only kisses he'd given were chaste good-night kisses after tucking her in to their king-size bed to sleep alone. There was no way in hell she was ruining this moment.

In fact...

Instinct and devilment mixed and meshed and Grace eased to her tiptoes. Holding his gaze, she pressed her mouth to his, while her heart thumped wildly against her chest. She moved her lips a little, tasting him, tantalizing him, and just when she thought he would completely ignore her, his eyelids drifted shut, his mouth came to life under hers and his arms tightened around her.

Chapter Eight

For Nick the world ceased to exist, except for the taste and feel of Grace. His hands slid along the curve of her torso and down the swell of her hips and he realized how perfectly sized she was. Her head reached his shoulder. Her body fit against his as if it were made to be there. And his hands fit her shape. But it was the alluring taste of her mouth that drew him. Soft and wet, it enticed him to come farther, taste more, give more, take more.

He felt himself being pulled under, swept away, and totally lost until a spark of sanity ignited in the back of his brain. First, he remembered that she'd probably come to Turner to divorce him. Then he remembered that was more than likely because there was another man. Then he remembered that once she got her memory back, she'd hate him.

She'd hate him. The mere thought hurt now. Before, when Grace was an abstract recollection from his past, he could deal with her hating him. He could even understand her hating him. But now that he knew her again, now that he'd spent time with her, tasted her, touched her, the thought that she would hate him pierced his heart.

Holding back a sigh of regret, and feeling an ache of misery so intense it felt more physical than emotional, Nick reached behind him for her hands, which she had fastened at his nape.

"Let's get back to the house."

"Why? Let's stand out here and kiss."

As she said the last, she nuzzled his neck and Nick gritted his teeth against the pain of wanting her. "Grace, you were very recently hurt. Today, you feel pretty good…"

Pretty good? God, she'd felt wonderful. She felt like every good thing he could want in life. She felt like heaven.

He cleared his throat. "Today, you're feeling well, and you want to try things that probably aren't in your best interest."

"Since when is kissing one's husband not in a woman's best interest?" She nipped his neck again. "I remember you telling me that you and I could lie on a blanket for hours and neck." As she said this, she pulled back to peer at him. "Well, it never struck me until this moment, but I can really understand that." She eased to her tiptoes, slid her arms around his neck and grazed his mouth with a soft, fleeting brush of her lips. "Anybody ever tell you you're a wonderful kisser?"

Nick cleared his throat. "Only you."

"That's because I have good taste."

Nick pulled her hands from behind his neck again. "And you also need to get into the house."

"Why?"

"Why? Grace, you're killing me." Not knowing how else to get himself out of this, Nick added, "If you don't stop, I'll be so aroused I'll be in pain for the next three days."

She grinned wickedly. "I know a way to ease that pain."

Squeezing his eyes shut, Nick said, "Grace, you're sick. You were just in an accident, you're not ready for any of this yet."

"I'm well," she said and brushed his lips again. "I feel terrific. And I'm ready. I swear I am."

Not knowing what else to do, Nick stepped away from her, grabbed her hand and began leading her to the house. "You've argued with me about everything since I brought you home. Just trust me on this one thing… Will you?"

Though it was difficult, Grace did not sulk through dinner. Her purpose was to win Nick back, not drive him farther away. For all she knew, sulking, pouting, demanding her own way might have been what drove them apart in the first place. Since she was determined to win him back, sulking and pouting had to go.

Besides, she had won some points that afternoon. She knew she aroused him. She knew he *wanted* her. And since most normal people typically took some time to get to know each other before they made love, Grace had to concede that she and Nick were moving too fast.

So she didn't pout. She didn't sulk. Instead, she enjoyed Stella's wonderful trout amandine and led Nick to the perfect conversational territory. His job. Not only did that serve the purpose of getting him to relax with her again, but it also helped her get to know him.

"One of the first companies I went into was run by idiots."

"Why don't you tell me how you really feel?" Grace teased with a laugh, lifting her wineglass from beside the elegant china Nick used. She knew it wasn't hers. She'd never choose something that fussy. She was tempted to ask him where he got it, but something told her not to. If she hadn't picked it out, maybe she didn't want to know who had.

"Well, you asked about my job, I'm telling you," Nick said, leaning back in his chair.

The dining room was a mix of pastel colors and dark mahogany furniture. The dusky table gleamed around white lace place mats. Candles provided the only light in the room.

"And I really want to know," Grace said. Hypnotized by the candlelight and the company, she leaned toward him. "So, go on and tell me about this group of idiots."

"The good news and the bad news was that the guy who put the company together had a gem of an idea. He hit the ground running and in his first five years of business had amassed an actual fortune. Once he'd made his millions, he took the company public and made himself another bundle by selling stock. Before it was all over, he'd become a multimillionaire in less than seven years."

"Wow," Grace said, solidly impressed. "What kind of company was this?"

"Trash," Nick said, then he laughed heartily. Grace smiled, listening to the music of his voice. "The man made his fortune collecting trash."

"There's a sort of poetic irony in that," she said.

"You bet there is," Nick agreed. "Even after going public, the corporation continued to grow, but as with a lot of good companies, the true test comes when a business gets too big for one man to handle alone."

Intrigued, Grace swirled the wine in her glass. "How so?"

"Well, first, there's the ability of the leader to give up power."

"And if the leader can't give up some of his control, the company goes down the tubes," Grace speculated, confused because she already knew that. Then she remembered she worked with Nick, for the same company about which he was telling her, so, of course, she'd understand the basic business principles he practiced.

"Precisely," he agreed. "Once a company reaches a certain size, it can't be run by one person. And if that person continues to try to run it alone, nine chances out of ten the company will fail."

He was silent for a second and Grace watched the play of the hazy light across his face. The dark shadows accenting his high cheekbones gave him a mysterious, forbidding look. Instead of being afraid, Grace found him to be incredibly sexy.

"The other side of the same problem is that when a seemingly common man becomes as successful as Chas became, he tends to think that if he can run a company, anybody can, so he can pull anyone in off the street to help him to continue to grow the business. In this particular case, rather than hiring experts, my company president hired his friends."

"That doesn't sound good."

"It's bad for two reasons. First, he needed accountants and business majors. He hired people who weren't properly trained. But, second, and sometimes even worse, his friends abused their power. They certainly abused their friendships."

"I see your point."

Again, Nick was silent for several seconds. Grace only watched him, sensing that what he was about to tell her was important, if only to him. Which meant that for the first time since her accident, he was going to tell her something truly personal. If she was lucky, she would be getting her first look into his soul.

"I worked for that company for only two weeks before I saw I was the only one who really knew my job. When I called the man who had hired me to scope out the problem and gave him the news, his first move was to oust the company president from the board of directors. Then he told Chas that as a condition to staying on as company president and retaining the ability to run his company, he had to fire his friends. He did, then I hired his new staff.''

Resting her chin on her closed fist, Grace studied Nick for several seconds. She watched the candlelight as it played across his cheekbones and glittered in his black hair. "It bothered you that time.''

He caught her gaze with his sharp brown eyes. "Only because Chas wasn't your normal corporate executive. He was so average, so common, that everyone thought he made his fortune because he was lucky. But he wasn't lucky. He was smart. Very, very smart. He made only one judgment error—hiring his friends—yet I had to *fight* to get my boss to allow him to keep his job.'' Nick paused, drew a long breath. "I lost sleep over that one.''

"He reminded you of yourself.''

Looking away, Nick clucked his tongue. "Even though he was a hundred pounds overweight and bald as an eagle, I saw myself in him.''

"And now?''

"Now, I don't take it so personally,'' he told her. "Now I know that for every overpaid executive I fire, there are probably three talented, deserving people who get hired. I also have the satisfaction of knowing that every company I save will still be in business five years from now. I don't see the jobs I take, Grace, only the jobs I save.''

He had a certain pride in his voice, and a warning. She could tell he saw himself as standing up for the little guy, and she wasn't sure if he was warning her off because her father was wealthy enough that she wasn't one of the "little people'' or if he was warning her off because he wanted her to be aware that he hadn't forgotten his roots. He'd slipped something very important when he told her about how she'd changed his perspective about college. He had been poor. She had come from money.

She would remember that.

"Come on, I'll walk you up to bed," Nick said, pushing away from the table.

When he came around to pull Grace's chair out for her, she protested. "But it's only nine-thirty."

"By the time you get yourself into pajamas, wash your face and brush your teeth, it will be ten."

She sighed. "I suppose."

"Would it help if I promised to read you a bedtime story?"

"Yes," she said with a laugh, and turned to find herself almost in his arms. She looked into his eyes and the air between them crackled. One step, one short step and she'd be flush against him. If she lifted herself on tiptoe, their lips would be brushing...

It was tempting, so tempting, but she'd learned her lesson that afternoon. Because she'd pushed, he'd backed away, and it had taken her most of dinner to get him to relax with her again.

She stepped away.

"Good night, Nick. I think I'll tuck myself in tonight."

Chapter Nine

After the way she'd tormented him on their walk the day before, Nick never thought he'd regret that Grace had decided to back away last night. But he did. He felt a jolt of pain when she told him she'd tuck herself in, but he reminded himself that was for the best.

When she seated herself at breakfast before he could jump from his chair to help her, Nick conceded that her obvious rejection—good though it was from most perspectives—was killing him. When she asked for some time alone after lunch, Nick became downright moody. Now, at dinner again, Nick felt as gangling and awkward as he had in high school.

The first time Grace had ever talked with him had been equal parts torment and pleasure. A tough guy in high school, he had all the right answers and knew all the right lines, but though Grace didn't belittle him or scoff at him, she wasn't one to be put off with platitudes. She talked with him and ignored him in random measures until eventually Nick didn't know if it was a talking day or an ignoring day. He dropped the cliché flirting, he dropped the trite lines, he dropped the tough-guy act, and he really talked with her.

He remembered the day as if it were yesterday. Because in a sense, it was. If he didn't know better, he'd think she did have her memory back. If she didn't, she had an instinctive man-woman strategy down pat and even amnesia couldn't take it away from her. In ignoring him, she was getting more of his attention than he'd actually planned to give her.

"That's a lovely dress," he said as he seated her for dinner.

"Thank you. It's funny. You'd think I'd remember buying something this pretty," she said, wrapping the flame-colored silk in her fist and filtering it through her fingers.

Unfortunately, that was as personal as Grace allowed the conversation to get. So, after dinner, Nick didn't ask if he could walk her to her room. He simply put his hand at the small of her back and guided her up the steps when the time came. She was quicker than he was when they got to the door, and though he hadn't planned on giving her a good-night kiss, he was unexpectedly miffed when she closed herself off in her room before he had the chance to be tempted.

He took a breakfast tray to her room the next morning, and, as he had in the hospital, he perched himself on the edge of the bed to watch her eat. She offered him her muffin. He refused, then wished he would have taken it when she moaned in ecstasy at the sweet taste and used her tongue daintily to prevent losing even the tiniest morsel.

Knowing he had to get out before he did something foolish like kiss her, Nick said, "Grace, one of the reasons I brought you breakfast in bed is that I wanted to spend some time with you now since I need to be in my office for most of the day.''

"Meeting with the man who gives you your assignments?" she asked casually.

"No, just straightening out some paperwork."

She tossed him a confused expression. "I thought that was my job."

"It is," he said without missing a beat, knowing she was too smart not to pick up on that. "But since you're not feeling well, I'll have to do it."

He said the words and drew a slow, quiet breath waiting for the bomb to fall. He started the countdown in his head.

Ten… She considered what he'd said.

Nine… She recognized he was keeping her away from her job.

Eight… She evaluated her own physical condition and decided she was well enough to do her own work.

Seven… She estimated whether or not she could win the argument with him.

Six… She planned a strategy so she *knew* she'd win the argument with him.

Five… She wondered why she should have to argue with him.

Four… She pumped herself by reminding herself that if that was her job, she had more right to go into the office than he did.

Three… She worked herself into a real tizzy over his dominating her.

Two… She reminded herself that no one dominated her.

One… She exploded.

Even as he said the word *one* to himself, Grace caught his gaze. He recognized the light in her beautiful pastel eyes and almost stepped back. But she shook her head slightly, picked up her muffin and said, "That's fine. I have some things I want to do around the house. I guess I'll see you at dinner, then."

Irritated, confused, confused because he was irritated, Nick drove to his office, but he didn't get a damn bit of work done. All he could do was think about Grace.

Yes, he knew it wasn't right for them to start any kind of a relationship. No, he didn't want to hurt her or be hurt when she regained her memory and left... But, damn it, he also didn't understand what was going on here. It was only when he realized that she might be ignoring him because she was *offended,* not pouting or angry, that Nick also began to feel guilty. So much for being attuned to her moods. She might have held a civil conversation with him at dinner the night after their excursion into the woods, but it had wounded her to be rejected by him.

And it pained him to have to reject her.

Sighing, he told himself he had no choice but to reject her. He stayed in his office until a quarter after six, just so he wasn't tempted to go home and entertain her, then he left and found a florist who stayed open after hours for men who needed flowers to apologize for working late, and he bought Grace a dozen roses.

When he pulled into his driveway, he saw that Stella's van was gone. His fist clenching and unclenching around the box of roses, Nick pondered the possibility that Grace had sent Stella away for a reason. Like she planned to try to seduce him again. It wouldn't surprise him that his overly nosy housekeeper would agree to help with the scheme. She would like nothing better than to play match-maker.

Calling himself a paranoid fool, he stepped out of his vehicle and started up the back steps to the kitchen. This way he could gauge Grace's mood, and if he suspected anything shady, he could ditch the flowers because he didn't want to give her the wrong idea.

Sneaking in through the garage entryway, he noticed an absolutely delicious scent and was glad that Stella had at least made dinner for them. He opened the kitchen door and tiptoed inside.

"What the hell are you doing?"

Grace couldn't have scared him more if she'd blown the question at him through a bullhorn. Grabbing his chest with one hand, he crushed the box of roses with the other and managed to regain his composure by dragging in long breaths of air.

"I was coming home from work," he responded irritably. "What the hell are *you* doing?" he added, referring to the fact that she was in the kitchen.

"Obviously, making dinner. One of Stella's grandkids took sick. I gave her the afternoon off."

"Oh," Nick said, chagrined. Here he stood, yelling at the woman who was kind enough to do a good deed for his housekeeper and was also making him dinner. He felt like an idiot. Luckily, he had flowers.

"Here, I bought you these."

It was the first real gesture of *affection* he'd given her since her accident, and tears welled in Grace's eyes. He'd been kind to her. He'd been good to her. He'd been more than considerate of her. But he'd never really given her any true sign of romantic love...until this.

She looked up at him and said, "Thank you." But the words were so difficult, her voice broke.

He combed his fingers through his thick, wavy hair. "Look, I'm really sorry if I seemed mean to you the other day," he said, and Grace watched him tuck his hands in his pockets as if he knew he had to do something drastic to keep from touching her. "It's just that you're sick..."

"I'm not sick," she said, and, again, her voice broke. If ever it was obvious that two people loved each other, it was her and Nick, but something had come between them. And tonight she intended to find out what it was— no matter how much he tried to deny it or change the subject—and no matter how much it hurt.

"For Pete's sake, Nick, I not only followed your house-keeper around out of boredom, I cleaned the kitchen, straightened my closets and made us dinner. These aren't the actions of an invalid, they're the actions of a very healthy woman. What do I have to do to you to prove that I'm perfectly fine?"

Uncomfortable, he nonetheless caught her gaze. "Have a memory?" he asked softly.

She shook her head angrily. "I can't do that. We both know I can't do that. But that doesn't mean I'm still sick. I think the bottom line is that there is something wrong with our marriage." She drew a deep breath for courage. "In fact, Nick, if I were a betting woman, I'd say the truth is that you don't love me anymore."

The room was draped in total silence for at least a minute. Grace waited, desperately hoping he'd give her some sign, some ray of light, that everything between them hadn't died. But in the final seconds of that minute, hope diminished into a misty vapor. Then, quietly, unexpectedly, he said, "I do love you, Grace."

"Really?" she answered. Unable to hold back her tears anymore, she began to cry. "You couldn't prove it by me. Did you know Dr. Ringer thinks I'm not getting my memory back because I don't *want* to get my memory back?"

Nick shook his head. "No, I didn't know that."

Choking on a sob, Grace nodded. "He thought there was something really wrong in my life, something I didn't want to face. But apparently you cured him of thinking that. Once he talked with you, he came into my room and practically insisted I go home because not only were we financially solvent, but you also told him we didn't argue."

Feeling ashamed, Nick said, "Grace, I'm sorry, I had no idea that he'd—"

"You had no idea you'd had such an impact on Dr. Ringer, or you had no idea that I'd already guessed we had marital troubles but was simply too ashamed to admit them to a stranger, even if he was my doctor, and—''

He cut her off before she could finish. Not just because he didn't want her to get upset in her precarious state of mind, but also because he couldn't stand to watch her in this much pain. ''Grace, what would ever make you think we're having marital problems?''

She lifted her chin defiantly. ''For one, you aren't sleeping with me.''

''Because you're sick.''

''I told you. I'm not sick. I'm well. In fact, I'd be a hundred percent better now if my husband was back in my bed.''

Nick might have been able to fight her if she hadn't been so distraught. As it was, this was the kind of situation Dr. Ringer had warned him to avoid, but her reaction was also the personification of Nick's worst fears.

In spite of her rapid physical recovery, Nick didn't think she was emotionally strong enough to handle the truth about their lives. Though the easy, obvious answer to every problem they'd had since she came to live with him would be to simply admit the truth, Nick genuinely believed Grace couldn't handle it. He didn't merely worry that the truth would shock her so much it would do emotional damage. He also worried that once she knew she wasn't living with Nick, Grace would simply leave, refuse any further help or care from him, and return to Angus's ranch alone.

And to an unknown fate.

Nick hadn't forgotten what the doctor had said about Grace's fear of going home. Though he hadn't wanted to discuss it with her, Nick's greatest purpose for keeping Grace with him, and away from the ranch, was to keep her from the real reason she wasn't getting her memory back—someone who might be hurting her.

And he couldn't risk telling her about that, either.

He had five days before Angus and Cal returned from Houston, which meant he probably had four nights at most when he'd have to sleep with her. That wasn't so bad. Surely, with ground rules, they could handle that. Anything was better than arguing with her while she sobbed.

"I'll sleep in the same bed with you as long as you promise you won't try to push us into something you're not ready for."

"You mean, you don't want to have sex."

"Grace, it isn't that I don't want to have sex," he said and almost groaned with the frustration of wanting it. "I really don't want to hurt you."

She took a long breath, closed her eyes and obviously considered that.

"All right," she said, sounding halfway between relieved and confused.

But Nick didn't have any confusion about this situation at all.

He was in trouble.

Deep, dark trouble.

Chapter Ten

They ate their dinner in near silence and cleaned up the kitchen together. When Grace excused herself to get ready for bed, Nick debated staying downstairs until he knew she was asleep, but he recognized she wouldn't accept that. So he went upstairs to the room he had been using, showered, shaved and put on the only pair of pajamas he owned—the ones his mother had bought him for Christmas.

He didn't question why he'd showered or shaved. He didn't question why he'd put on the pajamas instead of sweatpants. This was Grace...*Grace*...he was about to get into bed with. Even though he couldn't touch her, that didn't keep him from wanting to be the absolute best for her.

She wasn't in bed when he entered her room, but the bathroom door was closed and a crack of light shone beneath it. Nervous, and trying not to be, Nick decided the best course of action would be to behave normally.

He got under the covers, on his "side," and removed the novel he was reading from the top drawer of the bedside table. Accustomed to being alone, exactly like this in this bed, it took him only a minute before he was comfortably lost in the story, so it startled him when Grace opened the bathroom door.

But surprise gave way to regret when the door opened and Grace stood before him. The light of the room behind her nearly negated the filmy nightgown she wore. Despite the fact that it was floor-length, he could clearly see the silhouette of her body, shrouded in puffs and swirls of lavender.

He swallowed as a hundred sensations bombarded him. First, he clearly remembered their wedding night. Second, he wondered where the hell his mind had been when he'd bought her the nightgown that matched her eyes. Third, he just plain wanted her. Fourth, he was a hell of a lot stronger than he was at eighteen. She'd come seeking a divorce, could be promised to another man and deserved better than him anyway.

"Oh, you have the lamp on," Grace said innocently, peeking out of the bathroom to see that for herself. "I can just get the bathroom light and come to bed then."

Nick heard the nervousness in her voice and cursed himself for agreeing to this. But reminding himself that he was stronger than he'd been as a teenager, he said, "Relax, Grace." Pulling back the cover, he casually offered her the place in the bed beside him as if they'd done this a million times.

"I am relaxed," she said, then slid into bed.

To help normalize the situation, Nick went back to his reading. Grace pulled the cover over her, almost to her chin, and spent a few minutes trying to get comfortable.

Nick closed the book. "Does my light bother you?"

Looking at the ceiling, Grace answered, "I don't know. Does your light usually bother me?"

"No," Nick said, because his light couldn't bother a woman who lived a hundred miles away. Reaching over, he snapped it out anyway. He shifted the pillows he'd used to support his back while reading, tossed one out of the bed and then lay down beside her. The minute his back flattened on the mattress, he could feel how stiffly she was lying.

He sighed. "Grace, this is exactly why I didn't want to sleep with you. You're so nervous, neither one of us is going to get any sleep, and though I can function on a few hours a night, you can't. You're recovering."

She cleared her throat. "I'm not nervous."

"Really?" he asked, reaching under the covers. He grabbed her forearm, which was so taut it could have passed for wood. "Then what's this?"

"Would you believe I'm doing isometrics?"

He couldn't help it, he laughed. Game to the end. "No, I would not believe you're doing isometrics. But I would believe that you're nervous."

"Of course I am," Grace said. Anger overriding nerves, she shifted on the bed until she was facing him. Her violet eyes sought his in the darkness. "A decent husband would have done something to try to make me relax instead of pointing out that I was nervous as if it was a criticism."

He sighed. She was right. That's what he had done. "Okay. You're right. A decent husband probably would have found a way to help you relax. Come here," he said, and pulled her against him.

Her soft body molded against his, the silken skin of her bare arms slid along his palms, the frills and softness of her long nightgown tickled his feet. Right at that moment he thanked the Lord that his mother had bought him pajamas and that he'd had the foresight to wear them.

"Is that better?" he asked gently, stifling the urge to grit his teeth.

She sighed airily and nestled against him. "Yes. Much better." Silent again, she snuggled in more deeply.

Several seconds passed in torturous silence. He told himself he could handle the feel of the feminine garment as it billowed over the exposed skin of his hands and feet. He told himself that holding her against him was a sort of obligation. Keeping her healthy and safe as he waited for Angus's return was his way of redeeming himself for leaving her. He wouldn't let her softness, the feel of the wonderful curves of her body against his, or even her scent get to him. Then he told himself that if this lasted more than four nights he'd be a basket case.

He felt her slow, level breathing and thought she'd fallen asleep, until she said, "I really love you, Nick."

He wasn't sure why that came as such a surprise, but it did. A lump formed in his throat and tears burned his eyes. He really loved her, too. He really, really loved her, too.

He couldn't imagine how she was going to react when she found out the truth, but he knew with absolute certainty that she would be hurt. He wondered how things had gotten so far out of hand, then reminded himself that with Angus out of town, she had no one to care for her, so Nick had been gallant when he stepped in. He reminded himself that when she insisted on going home, he couldn't send her to her real home because she had a fear of some sort. Because he didn't know what she was afraid of, or of whom she was afraid, he couldn't tell her the truth and send her off to an unknown fate...

And, he reminded himself, if he had told her the truth at any point, she would have kicked him out of her life and he wouldn't have been able to protect her.

That's how they'd gotten here. And if one of them or both of them ended up getting hurt, he still felt that was a better alternative than sending her off to a potentially dangerous situation.

Sleepily snuggling against him, Grace murmured, "I don't remember you at all, but when we're like this...

when you kiss me or hold me, I know that we belong together.''

Squeezing his eyes shut, Nick bit his bottom lip.

That's exactly what he'd felt the night he married her.

They awakened spooned together like longtime lovers, or like a couple who really had been married for ten years. In a half-awake state, Nick felt Grace turn in his arms, then gently pepper his face with kisses. First his forehead, then his eyelids, his cheeks, and his chin. Instinctively, he sought her lips with his own, and his hands ran from her shoulders, down her torso and across her soft derriere.

But as the kiss and the movement brought him into clearer consciousness, he remembered all the reasons he had no right to be kissing her or holding her so intimately. He also remembered that in the last minutes before he drifted off to sleep, he finally figured out a way to find Angus. Which meant, by this time tomorrow, she might be gone.

He pulled away as tactfully as he could and got out of bed.

He made the mistake of pausing to look at Grace—still half-asleep, her mouth still dewy from kisses, her hair still tousled across the pillow—and the temptation to return nearly overwhelmed him.

''Where are you going?'' she asked dreamily.

He cleared his throat. ''To shower. I need to go back into work today.''

''Oh,'' she said, obviously disappointed. ''I'd hoped we could spend a little time together.''

Unable to resist, he sat beside her on the bed and took her hands. ''We will,'' he said. Because he'd figured out a way to find Angus, this might be his last day with her and he wanted at least a few more hours of happiness. Since he hadn't given in to temptation the night before,

Nick was feeling fairly strong, fairly confident, like a man who didn't have anything to worry about...

Except another night of sleeping with her, if his plan didn't work out.

But his plan probably would work out. He wasn't going to the office because of work but to call Angus's ranch. From what Nick remembered, Angus didn't have an outside office, only the office at the ranch, but he had a secretary. Every time before this when Nick had called, he'd called at night. It dawned on him, right before he fell asleep last night, that maybe if he called the ranch in the morning, he'd find the secretary. It also occurred to him that if he didn't find Angus's secretary at the ranch, Nick could ask the housekeeper if Angus had left his secretary's number, or ask if the number wasn't available somewhere, like in an address file on the desk in the office.

Once he explained his dilemma to the secretary, he was sure she'd get word to Angus to call him or get the message about Grace to Angus herself, and once Angus got the message, Nick knew wild horses wouldn't keep him from Grace.

Unfortunately, that meant today might be his last day with her. And selfish though that was, Nick planned on having that day. He planned on pulling out all the stops. They'd take a long walk, they'd make a fire, they'd have a romantic dinner... As long as Stella was around to keep everything in line, Nick knew he could have his one day of ecstasy.

"I'm all yours from the minute I get back from the office," he began, but the phone on the bedside table trilled.

Nick reached for the phone. "Hello?"

"Hey, kid, this is Stella. My grandson's got the chicken pox. He can't go back to school until he loses all his spots. Can you do without me for two or three days? My daughter-in-law can't afford the time off work."

"Yeah, sure, no problem," Nick said automatically.

Sitting up, Grace asked, "Who was that?"

Nick smiled at her. "Stella," he answered casually. "She can't come over today because her grandson is sick…"

Stella. He'd planned on using Stella as a chaperon of sorts.

Grace stretched to reach him and planted a soft kiss on his lips. "You're very sweet."

Her constant trust in him not only amazed Nick, it also gave him a sort of cautionary reminder. He took her hands from his neck. "No, Grace, I'm not sweet. That's the kind of arrangement Stella and I have worked out. It's loose and informal, and the only way she'd come to work for me. She's also the only housekeeper I'd let in my home full-time."

"Why?" Grace asked around a confused laugh. "Nick, you always act as if you have something to hide…"

"I have plenty to hide, Grace. Everybody has something that they hide. Even you, if we got right down to it, probably have something in your life that you don't want anyone else to know."

"Do you think so?" she asked innocently, naively, then rose to her knees and put her arms around his neck again. "Maybe I did something really, really wrong. Maybe that's why I'm not getting my memory back."

Nick held back a groan. "Grace, don't. I'm not the person you should be talking with about this."

"Don't be silly," Grace admonished. "I love you. I always have. I may not remember…"

Angry now, Nick snapped, "Grace, don't be so naive. Don't be so open. Maybe *I'm* the one person you *shouldn't* be trusting right now."

With that, he rose from the bed and walked out of the room, grateful that his clothes were in a different bedroom and suddenly grateful that in another day this charade would finally be over.

Chapter Eleven

When Nick emerged from his room, showered and fully dressed, he debated going back into Grace's room to check on her, but he decided not to. Things had gone too far, too fast. They were out of control. It was one thing to want to keep her safe, protect her, care for her until Angus returned, and even give himself one good day to remember her by. It was quite another thing to let her believe in him with that damn blind trust of hers when she didn't remember how he'd hurt her.

Intending to make a pot of coffee before he left, Nick jogged down the steps and walked to the kitchen. When he pushed open the door, not only did the scent of fresh coffee greet him, but the aroma of French toast hit him too.

"I don't have time for breakfast."

"You need breakfast," Grace said emotionlessly. "With your being as angry as you are with me, you'll stay at work longer than the morning. You'll probably skip lunch and get home at about the time I'm starting dinner, and you'll tell me you'll wait for dinner, which will mean you'll go at least another hour without food. So eat.''

She set the plate of French toast on the table, which she'd set with silver and everyday dishes, and Nick looked at them. Such simple, yet such important gestures of basic human love. He didn't deserve any of this in spite of the fact that she was right. She was angry, and she was right. He wouldn't have lunch, and without Stella around to chaperon, he didn't think it would be smart for him to come home before dinner, so he needed breakfast.

Regardless, he didn't think it was wise for them to be in the same room together again until they cooled off. A compromise was in order. "I'll be home before lunch," he said and started for the door. When she gave him a disbelieving look, he added, "I promise."

When he was gone, Grace sat down on one of the captain's chairs beside the round table. She knew what he was doing and still he hurt her.

She couldn't believe she could be so thin-skinned and wondered how she'd win him back if she couldn't handle the resistance she knew she would encounter when they got this close. In only another minute of hugging and kissing this morning, Grace recognized they would have been well on their way to making love.

Nick hadn't rejected her because he didn't want her. He'd rejected her because their relationship was a mess. She couldn't get him to talk about it with her, so she'd chosen an unorthodox path. She'd chosen to get him to love her, to really, truly and completely love her, before they confronted the past. She'd never for one moment thought that that past wouldn't rear its ugly head and block her way. She'd never for one moment believed this journey was going to be easy.

Strengthened by her logic, she rose from the table, tossed the cold French toast into the disposal and began washing the dishes and planning lunch.

He might hurt her, but he wasn't going to deter her. She knew his pain was the biggest part of their problem. She'd work around it. She'd plow through it. She'd completely ignore it if she had to, but one way or another, she was going to get him to see that the woman he was dealing with now was much different than the one who'd hurt him. Once he knew that, then maybe, just maybe, they could face his pain together.

Nick waited while Angus's housekeeper flipped through the entries in his card file. It was the first time in his life Nick could remember being glad that someone *didn't* use computers to their fullest advantage. If Angus weren't so old-fashioned, his phone numbers and addresses would be on his computer and probably under a password, not handwritten. As it was, with everything right out in the open on index cards, Nick still had at least a slim chance of getting Angus's secretary's name.

"The only secretary I remember Angus having," he told the housekeeper, "was a woman named Renee Jacobs. She'd worked for him for ten years before I got to know Angus, and, as loyal as she was, I'm going to assume she's still working for him."

"Here's a Jacobs," Angus's housekeeper announced.

"Is it Renee?"

"No, it's Russell."

"Might be her husband," Nick speculated and asked for the number. Angus's housekeeper gave Nick the number without so much as a second thought, and though Nick was grateful, he couldn't help thinking, as he had the first time he'd talked to the man, that this guy wasn't going to last very long in Angus's employ.

The second he disconnected the call, Nick began dialing the Jacobs residence. An older woman answered on the second ring. "Is this Renee Jacobs?"

"Yes, it is. May I ask who's calling?"

"Mrs. Jacobs, you probably don't remember me, but I'm Nick Spinelli. I dated Angus MacFarland's daughter, Grace Wright, in high school."

"Well, Nicki Spinelli! Of course I remember you. How are you?"

"I'm fine, Mrs. Jacobs, but I have a little problem and I need to get in touch with Angus MacFarland. He went out of town, apparently had some business in Houston, and though I've called every hotel in Houston, I haven't been able to get a desk clerk to give me his room number or to connect me to his room."

"Oh, I'm sorry, Nick, but I can't help you. I haven't worked for Angus for three years. Russ and I retired."

Nick sighed heavily. "I'm sorry to have bothered you. My business with Angus is rather important and when your number was in his card file, I just assumed you were working for him."

"Still get invited to his barbecues, but don't work for him," Renee announced blithely. "But I would be happy to try to scare him up for you...if your business is that important."

"Actually, it's not business, it's personal, and it's *very* important."

"Okay, Nick, let me see what I can do."

Instead of feeling better when he disconnected the call, Nick felt worse. No, what he felt was angry. Almost furious that fate had dropped Grace in his lap, teasing him, taunting him, but refusing to let him have her. The range of emotions he experienced was very similar to the feelings he'd had when he first went to California. Fate had dangled the perfect friend, the perfect mate, the perfect lover in front of his nose and quickly snatched her away.

And now, as if once wasn't enough, fate was teasing him again.

Grace wasn't sure why, but she almost expected Nick to be drunk when he came home. She never knew him to drink. Even at dinner with her now, he only had a glass of wine…and then only one. He never went for a second.

When Nick walked in the door that night, cold sober, and still angry, she was equal parts grateful and confused.

"Since I wasn't really sure when you'd be home, I didn't go to any real trouble for supper. I have a salad in the refrigerator and a plate of cold cuts."

Looking tired, Nick ran his hand down his face.

"Grace, I'm sorry I didn't come home to spend time with you like I'd promised, but something came up."

"That's all right," she said cheerfully, not intending to kill him with kindness but also not wanting to be a nagging, miserable wife. It was true they hadn't parted on the best of terms that morning and true he'd promised her the afternoon, but he ran a business—they ran a business—and even though she couldn't remember a darned thing about that business, she did have an instinct about not only the responsibilities of running your own company but meeting them. "I understand."

"Don't be nice to me, Grace," Nick growled, then walked over to the sink to wash his hands.

"Do you want me to yell at you, Nick?"

"I'd much rather that you be honest with me."

"I am being honest with you. True, I was disappointed that we couldn't spend the day together. True, you promised that we would. But equally true is that I somehow understand. You run a business. You've given up nearly two weeks of work to care for me. I can't complain about that."

"You could, Grace," Nick snapped. "You could complain about a lot of things. So why don't you just go ahead and complain and let's get it over with."

She wondered if this argument was an example of what was wrong with their relationship. But instead of having that usual sense that she'd done something and driven him away, Grace got a flash of insight that maybe the reason Nick had been so good to her through her recovery was to make up for his guilt over whatever it was that *he'd* done to destroy their marriage.

Suddenly that seemed so much more logical. It also explained the anger. It was almost as if he wanted her to punish him.

"I'm not going to fight with you just because you're in the mood for a battle."

"I'm not in the mood for a battle," he growled, and stormed to the refrigerator. He whipped out the bowl of salad and the plate of cold cuts she'd so lovingly prepared and tossed them to the round table.

"Yes, you are. Look at you!"

"All right, fine. So I'm in the mood to yell. So what?"

"So there's no reason to," Grace said calmly, gently.

As if realizing he was being obnoxious, he sighed heavily. Just looking at him, Grace felt the weight of his guilt as clearly as if she shared it. "Nick," she entreated softly. Even if he'd been a workaholic who'd ignored her—and she suspected that might have been their problem—he'd shown her another side of himself during her recuperation. If nothing else, he deserved a chance. From his reaction to her in bed that morning, she knew he wanted it.

"Whatever you've done, Nick. I forgive you."

He threw the bread on the table. "You forgive me?" he asked incredulously. "You forgive me? How the hell do you even know what you're forgiving me for?"

"I don't care what I'm forgiving you for. I told you before that I believed we had marital problems. Your behavior confirms that. So, now I'm forgiving you so that we can start over again."

"Thank you, Sigmund Freud."

His insulting tone went through her like a knife, but

she ignored it. "I'm not going to fight with you. I love you."

He squeezed his eyes shut. "Don't love me," he demanded miserably.

Taking advantage of the fact that he wasn't looking at her, Grace walked over and stood directly in front of him. "I love you. I *want* to love you. I don't care what went wrong. I don't care what you did wrong. I think we can straighten it out."

"Don't," he begged. "You don't know what you're saying."

"Why? Because you feel it's impossible to be forgiven?" she asked, taking the one step that separated them and putting herself flush against him. "I love you," she said again, then stretched on tiptoe until she could brush her lips across his. "I love you."

It was all too much for Nick. Her nearness and her willingness were overpowering, but she was also saying all the words he needed to hear. Intoxicating him with possibilities when he was vulnerable with the pain of knowing he was about to lose her again.

He was so frustrated. Renee hadn't been able to find Angus, either. She'd worked all day, calling her usual sources, using her Texas charm and her friendship and past professional relationship with Angus, trying to get anyone to put her through to Angus or to give him the message that she needed him to call her, but either Angus had disappeared from the face of the earth or he and Cal were staying with friends. Nick had remained in the office all day, pacing, prowling, waiting for Renee's call, and now, not only had he broken the promise to spend time with Grace, he wasn't any further ahead of the game. In his desperation, he'd explained to Renee about Grace's accident and asked her, if she did get in touch with Angus, to fill him in on the whole story.

Tortured because he needed to find Angus and end this

charade, he tried to push Grace away, and when he gripped her upper arms his fingers curled around them with determination, but his touch softened and he found himself pulling her against him.

Inside there was a broken man who sometimes believed he only invented her love for him and who needed not only to hear what she had to say, but who also needed to feel, physically, that he hadn't imagined that she loved him.

Before she could utter a word of protest, he scooped her off the floor and carried her up the steps to their flowery bedroom.

windows, her grief in plain view. Sorry that when he
gasped, she faced away, he let his mind return to how
their conversation, on the road, seemed to leave Nick
worried about his present fate.

He knew that it would take only seconds for him to
hoist her into his arms and throw all their problems
into the past. What she had wanted, because she needed it,
really, wistfully, until he made a judgment that she knew
more.

Before she could utter a spoken protest, he assured
her of his deep and carnal lust by the sheer reality of his
own indulgence.

Chapter Twelve

He'd been right about the way she'd look in his bed.

Though he was angry, Nick intended to be gentle, but
when he laid her down on top of the almond, mauve and
wine-colored spread, the tones surrounding her made her
skin appear pearlescent, luminous. Spread out atop the
bedcover, blending with the shades beneath her, her hair
became as rich and luxurious as the hues of the wet earth
in a hidden forest. Her eyes glowed like two violets, unexpectedly growing in the darkness. Their expression told
him that she knew exactly what they were doing, and it
was what she wanted. Maybe even what she needed.

Looking at her, his breathing became ragged, his pulse
raced. Impatience overcame him and he virtually tore the
buttons from his shirt.

When his shirt was gone, he knelt beside her on the
bed, bending down so he could skim his lips across hers
as he began working the fasteners of her shirt. But she
pulled his face down and kissed him with an intensity of
purpose so clear and so pure that reality began to slip
away and only sensation remained.

For Nick, the lines between right and wrong blurred and all that existed was need. Her lips were warm and greedy beneath his. Her hands came to life, searching for and finding his belt buckle. Even as he sought to satisfy her, pushing aside the material of her shirt to skim his fingers along the heated flesh beneath it, he ignited his own desires until the barriers of clothing between them were gone and they tumbled together across the riot of floral colors and lost themselves in each other and their needs.

He wasn't easy and he wasn't gentle. She didn't seem to want him to be. He forgot her injuries. She forgot they didn't really know one another. All she could think of was that she loved this man and he hurt. He ached. Whatever was wrong between them might not be solved by making love, but making love appeared to be able to ease some part of his pain. The strength of his passion, his hunger, reminded her of someone too long denied solace, or comfort, or maybe even simple human kindness.

She gave and gave and he took and took, until somehow their roles reversed and she found herself taking from him. She heard little whimpers of surrender and knew they were her own, knew she was begging him to take them the final steps, and wondered if he would listen or if, at the last second, he'd change his mind.

But Nick was too far gone for a sane decision. For the past fourteen years of his life Grace had represented everything that was feminine to him. Deep down inside he'd always known she was his other half, and though he'd shared physical relationships with other women, no other woman was Grace and no other relationship could satisfy him mind, body and soul.

He pressed himself into her, too steeped in his desire to please her and to satisfy his own need, to realize that when this was over, their world would be different. Instead, he let the desperation take him. He let twenty minutes of pure emotion ease the pain of ten years of separation, albeit temporarily. He took the burst of physical release as his due. He savored it. He reveled in it. Then he rolled onto his back, pulling Grace with him, and wondered how the hell they were going to get past this.

Grace gently laid her arm across his chest to hug him. "You took me like a starving man."

"I was a starving man," he said and felt his lips tremble. God, he had screwed up everything right from the beginning of this relationship because it was a relationship that wasn't meant to be. And now he'd made love to her again. He hadn't just set her up for a great deal of pain once Angus got home and her father helped her to get her memory back. He'd set himself up for the heartache of a lifetime—as if living through losing her the first time hadn't been torture enough.

He squeezed his eyes shut and laid his forearm over them, desperately trying to think of a way out of this and knowing there wasn't one.

"Care to tell me why you're starving?"

Her question was gentle, and kind, and altogether too innocent. It actually brought tears to Nick's eyes.

"Grace, I have a past that you can't possibly understand, and that time and distance won't heal." He paused for only a second, debating how honest he should be with her, and in the end decided she was not only strong enough to hear the truth, she deserved to know it. If what she told him the night before was any indication, she'd already guessed most of it anyway.

As far as keeping her here was concerned, he'd think of something. He had to think of something. He refused to let her go home to someone who might be hurting her.

"My past is what broke us up in the first place and it's what will keep us apart now."

He felt her swallow, and when she spoke, he could hear

in her voice that she was fighting her own tears. "I think I should at least get to hear about it."

"Hearing it won't change anything for you, because in the end it was a decision of mine that broke us up. So the fault is mine and the end result is going to be the same..."

"But it wouldn't hurt for me to hear it," Grace insisted softly. "It also might help for you to say it."

Though he didn't necessarily agree that it would help for him to say it, Nick did agree that she had a right to know the truth, and drew a long, resigned breath. "My father beat me and my mother regularly," he said calmly, almost casually, as if this was something you talked about over a backyard fence.

He felt Grace's indrawn breath and rushed ahead with his explanation before she had a chance to pity him. "He was an alcoholic, and though he couldn't hold a job, didn't make enough money to put food on the table or pay the bills, and seemed to take great delight in physically hurting both me and my mother, my mother absolutely adored him."

"That bothered you?"

"Oh, God, yes," Nick admitted and felt a tear escape from the corner of his eye and slide down his temple. Luckily, it was the side away from Grace. "First, I couldn't understand how she could adore a man who would hurt her," Nick said quietly but firmly. Then, a little more softly, a little more carefully, he added, "Second, I couldn't understand how she could adore somebody who would hurt me."

Grace felt his pain as if it were a living, breathing creature in the room with them. Cursing in her thoughts, she prayed for a memory, a recollection of what their life together had been like so that she could understand. But she got nothing. Not a glimmer of anything. Not a recollection of a problem. Not even an instinct. She prayed she hadn't been insensitive to his trouble. But from her own dealings with Nick over the past week, she also knew that if she had been insensitive, it would have been because he hid his pain, not because she refused to see it.

She said nothing, not really knowing how to comfort him, and realized the very best she could do was to accept what he told her and acknowledge his feelings. Lord knew, she'd never be able to understand it.

"We lost our electricity more times than I could count," he told her. "We rarely had phone service. I hid all that from you and everybody else by wearing a leather jacket and talking like a guy who belonged in reform school."

Grace eased herself more securely against him, offering consolation in the only way she could. She'd been right about her own insensitivity. If Nick wanted to hide something, she knew him well enough now to realize he would have succeeded.

"When I left my parents' home, I did it because they wanted me out. It was almost as if, once I became a man, I became competition for my dad.

"So, I left, went to California and put myself through college by working as a waiter."

Something about that struck Grace as odd. Not exactly wrong, but not exactly right, either. It was the closest she'd come to a memory since her accident, and the clarity of the feeling was so intense it sat on the edge of an actual fact but refused to budge even one step further. Frustrated, Grace nearly wept with the physical pain of trying to force something mental, but for Nick's sake she said nothing, didn't even react to her own loss, and focused on him as he continued to speak.

"My dad died about a week after I graduated from college," Nick reported softly. "My mother fell apart. Pretending to sympathize with her, I packed her up and moved her to Dallas, where she has relatives. In spite of the fact that my father is the one who kept her from her family, and in spite of the fact that she appears happier now than she had at any other time in her life, to this day, her living room is a virtual shrine to a man who nearly killed her twice.''

"I'm sorry," Grace whispered, nestling against him.

"I'm sorry, too," Nick said and went perfectly quiet. Now that the story was out, he felt clean somehow. He didn't even realize he'd felt dirty, but now that the story was out, there was no mistaking that he felt clean. He drew two long, slow breaths, more or less taking inventory of how he felt and suddenly knew that though he'd just told his secret to Grace, the world hadn't ended. He was still the same person he was before he started speaking... His father couldn't hurt him anymore.

"Oh, Grace," he said, squeezing his eyes shut and pulling her tightly against him. "I am so sorry."

"Don't be sorry. You needed to talk about that. I needed to hear it." She snuggled against him. "I'm glad you told me."

He shook his head. "That's not what I'm talking about. I might have needed to tell you and you might have needed to hear it, but this wasn't the way," he said, gesturing to indicate that they were in bed together and they had made love.

"I'm not sorry that we made love."

"I am," Nick said and Grace could tell he meant it, not because he was selfish or cruel but because in his misplaced sense of chivalry he believed that this would somehow hurt her.

"I can't see what you've done that would be so bad that I'd hate you," Grace said, desperate to ease his pain and equally desperate not to lose him. "But whatever it is, I've already told you that I would forgive you anything."

"I'm not going to hold you to that," Nick said, then eased her down so that she was lying flat and he could look down at her. "Grace, before you go making promises you can't keep, you should understand that I—"

She put her index finger over his lips to silence him. "You've gone through too much already for one night," she said, but she also knew her motives were much more selfish than that. If he told her everything, there was a very real possibility she would lose him tonight.

She didn't believe there was anything he could have done that could cause her to withhold forgiveness. But she knew Nick much better now than she had even an hour ago and she knew beyond a shadow of a doubt that he wasn't going to let her forgive him.

Which meant, once the secret was out, he'd be gone.

That was what she'd sensed all along. That was the way she sensed she'd lose him. That was why she always knew it was trouble to get her memory back, why she knew that if she went home, he wouldn't be with her.

Physically they might have lived together for nearly a decade, but emotionally they were miles apart.

Chapter Thirteen

As he expected, Nick was filled with remorse and regret the next morning. But what he hadn't expected was to feel as if a burden had also been lifted from his shoulders. Oddly, though he hadn't explained everything to Grace, he did have the relief that comes from confession. He felt so good that he genuinely believed that if she'd let him tell the rest of the story, he'd have complete closure. And maybe he could get on with the rest of his life.

Unfortunately, there were two complications to that. First, getting on with the rest of his life meant getting on without Grace, because no matter what she said, forgiving him wasn't going to be as easy as she thought. Second, she wasn't going to let him tell her.

Overwhelmed with love for her, he slid his arms under her still-sleeping form and pulled her against him, savoring her warmth, her softness. She'd given him a great gift the night before by listening without criticism, without demanding to know details he hadn't revealed, without belittling his pain by pretending it was unimportant because it was in the past or by pretending to understand when she couldn't understand. No one could.

She'd given him the chance to be whole again. And she'd done it as selflessly as the eighteen-year-old woman he'd married.

But she'd also done it with a maturity that eighteen-year-old Grace hadn't possessed. Last night, Grace had listened without pity, without anger, without any emotion at all, really, save for compassion, save for the desire to let him tell his story so he could be free of his demons.

"Good morning," Grace said, stretching beside him as she awakened.

"Good morning," Nick said and impulsively kissed her forehead. She didn't know, she *couldn't* know the gift she'd given him the night before. "Grace, I want to thank you for listening to me last night."

"My pleasure," she said casually.

He wouldn't let her dismiss the episode so easily, so lightly. "No, I mean it," he said, holding her firm when she would have rolled away from him. "What you did for me last night meant a great deal to me. You didn't judge or pretend to know more about what I was telling you than what I was telling you. I would have hated it if you'd pitied me. It would have been foolish for you to try to understand. What you said, what you did last night was perfect."

Searching his eyes, Grace was silent for a few seconds. Then she blew out her breath on a soft sigh and said, "Nick, I can't imagine living with an abusive parent. You undoubtedly went through hell. It was probably beyond understanding, and you're right, it would be foolish of me to try to understand. I don't remember what my childhood was like, but it must have been good..."

"It was good," Nick agreed, happy to change the subject now that he'd said his piece. "It was very good. That's why you're so good."

This time it was Grace who impulsively kissed him. "Oh, Nick, you're good, too. You're wonderful. Trust me, from the vantage point of someone who literally doesn't know you because I can't remember you, I saw just how kind and generous you are from the ways you cared for me."

Though he didn't want to do it, Nick knew they had to get out of bed before they again started something that wasn't in either of their best interest, though it was exactly what both of them wanted right now.

Time and distance might have made it easier to talk about his life, and he and Grace might also be mature enough to face the problems brought on by his childhood, but Nick couldn't ignore the fact that he not only left Grace ten years ago, he hadn't had courage enough to face her when he left. In an abstract way, she might be able to forgive that. But when she got her memory back, when the situation was more real than someone else's rendition of events, and she remembered the heartache he'd caused her, forgiving him would be impossible.

"Let's go make breakfast," he said, and began to slide out of bed.

She pushed him back down. "I'll get breakfast," she insisted, sitting up. Splendid in her nakedness, she rose from the bed and slid into a robe she had lying across the back of the Queen Anne chair Stella had insisted on buying for the room. She cinched the belt of the pink satin garment and started for the door. Because the robe had only one thin rope holding it at its center, Grace's legs were exposed with every step she took. The soft pink material molded to her body and clung to her bottom.

She opened the door and blew him a kiss before she left the room and Nick fell to his pillow, squeezing his eyes shut.

How would he ever live without her...?

Worse, how would he deal with seeing her pain first-hand when she got her memory back.

She brought him breakfast in bed. Damning any possible crumbs to hell, she set a tray between them and invited him to sit up and share muffins, coffee, scrambled eggs and bacon. He did so, reluctantly. Already they were too close. The physical attraction was hard enough to handle, but now she was becoming like a friend...no, more like a real lover.

This, he decided, looking around the flowery bedroom he'd created for her, was what true intimacy was all about. Casual closeness. Sharing food. Sharing thoughts. Being damn glad just to be in the other's company. And knowing, with absolute certainty, that you could say anything, express any opinion to your lover, and if they didn't understand they'd accept it.

"Apple butter is really very good," Grace insisted, trying to slather some across his English muffin.

He pulled it away in the nick of time. "You eat it for breakfast, lunch and dinner for three months then tell me it's God's gift to toast."

Grace couldn't help it, she laughed, then kissed him. "Finish your coffee," she ordered as she headed for the bathroom. "After I shower and dress, I'll take the tray downstairs."

Nick sat exactly as he was for at least five minutes after she left. She'd laughed at him, basically she'd laughed at his past, and it hadn't hurt. It felt good. It felt very good to not only laugh at the past, but to almost belittle it.

He rolled out of bed and took the tray downstairs, unconcerned about his nakedness since they were alone. Then he jogged up the steps, taking some two at a time to get his own shower and get back downstairs as quickly as possible. First, because he'd run out of convenient excuses for going into the office and he had to stay home today. Second, because there was still a possibility Renee would call.

Which meant today might be the day he lost Grace, and he didn't want to waste a minute of it.

Already lonely, Nick showered and dressed in worn jeans and an oversize college sweatshirt. While changing, he decided that if Renee found Angus, Nick couldn't simply dump the news on Grace. He knew he needed to prepare her, and felt the best way to do that would be to explain that he'd figured out an avenue for locating Angus.

"Hi," she greeted as he entered the kitchen. Up to her elbows in bubbles, Grace was washing their breakfast dishes.

"Hi," he returned, walking to the sink. "You know I have a dishwasher. You don't have to clean those things the hard way."

"I like to wash dishes," she said and pulled her hands from the water, examining the bubbles that clung to her fingers as if they were diamonds. "Isn't that odd?"

"No," Nick said, then began storing the unused muffins and jellies from breakfast. "Simple chores are soothing chores."

When he picked up the dish towel to help her, Grace angled her chin toward his movement and said, "Does that mean you're in need of a little soothing?"

He laughed. "No. I'm trying to be helpful. I feel fine. Great, actually."

"Good, then you won't mind if we do something special today."

He peered at her. "Like what?"

"I have a sudden, intense desire to go antiquing."

"You're kidding," he said, half-fearful, half-confused. Both for the same reason. For all he knew, she could be an antique dealer. He couldn't risk them running into someone she'd know any more than he could risk missing

Renee's call. Considering both of those risks, he decided there was no time like the present to tell her about his efforts to find her father.

"Actually, Grace, we have to stay around the house because I'm expecting a call."

"Oh," she said, sounding disappointed. "Can't the answering machine get it?"

"Well, I'm expecting a call from someone who has spent the last twenty-four hours trying to track down your father."

That stopped her. This time her "Oh" was filled with appreciative surprise.

"I don't want you being without your family any longer. We both know you're not going to get your memory back with me—" he drew in a long, tortured breath "—since you now understand that you don't live with me, and nothing around here is going to stimulate your memory."

He glanced at Grace, and though she wouldn't look at him, she nodded.

"You need to see and be with your family."

"Yeah," Grace said, staring at the bubbles in the dishwater. From her tone, Nick could tell that Grace also knew that once her family arrived, they'd be taking her with them. She wouldn't be staying.

She didn't want to go. He could see it in the dejected set of her shoulders. He could hear it in her voice. Though Nick accepted that he'd done the right thing, he still felt like a heel. He also hurt every bit as much as she did. The rest of his life yawned before him like a long, black abyss, interrupted only by short bursts of intense, pressure-filled work.

The room grew so silent the only sound was the tick of the clock above the entryway.

"We still have the day, though. We could make it special,'' Grace quietly suggested, reminding Nick that he had wanted one good day with her to hold dear for those times when he'd be tempted to wonder if she was real or a figment of his imagination.

Chapter Fourteen

"So, how do you suggest we spend the day?" Grace asked cautiously.

But Grace realized that this last day was actually a gift they were giving each other. Nick wasn't the only one who'd need a good memory for down times. Because unless she could think of something, this time tomorrow they might be alone again.

Only now she hurt worse for Nick being alone than she did for herself.

"There's not much to do up here in the mountains," Nick admitted. "And we can't leave because I don't want to miss your father's call."

"What's the new way you found to track him down?"

"I called the ranch and got the name of his secretary... Well, Renee isn't your father's present secretary. She's retired now, but she still knows all Angus's favorite spots and she's still got her southern charm working for her. One way or another, she should find your father."

"But not necessarily today?" Grace asked, her spirits lifting.

Nick shook his head. "No. Not necessarily today, but Renee's smart and persistent. I wouldn't count her out, either."

Grace didn't remember Renee from squat, so she couldn't make any educated guesses about the woman's persistence or abilities. But Grace did realize that Nick, a very smart, determined man, had been trying to locate her father for nearly two weeks and he hadn't been successful. Odds were that Renee wouldn't have any more luck than Nick had had.

Believing that she had at least a day, maybe two or three, to continue to force Nick into realizing their relationship wasn't doomed, Grace happily said, "Since we're stuck in the house, and our options are limited, I think we should do something completely outrageous."

Nick eyed her skeptically. "Like what?"

"Let's cook."

He'd expected to have to argue her out of spending the day sunk beneath bubbles in his oversize oval tub. When she didn't suggest anything even remotely romantic, her answer took him completely by surprise.

"Cook?"

"Cook."

"What do you want to cook?"

"How about fourteen-hour spaghetti sauce?"

"Fourteen-hour spaghetti sauce?" he parroted incredulously.

"Any Italian cookbook worth its salt will have a really detailed, time-consuming recipe for spaghetti sauce...and I saw that Stella had a cookbook for Italian food in the pantry. So, what do you say? Are you in? Will you help me make sauce?"

"I don't know, Grace. I don't think this is such a good idea."

"Why not?"

"Because I don't want to be left holding the bag with

this stuff. What if your father calls after only seven hours of your fourteen-hour sauce?''

''We'll invite him to dinner.''

Her pragmatic answer made him laugh, and Nick realized how foolish it was to be concerned about a few wasted tomatoes and some spices. ''All right. We'll make spaghetti sauce.''

They didn't find a recipe for a fourteen-hour sauce, only for a sauce that took eight hours, but Grace was completely satisfied. Cookbook in hand, she pillaged Nick's cupboards and refrigerator for the appropriate ingredients and spices. Then she went to work.

''You are really good at this,'' Nick observed, watching as she sautéed her diced ingredients. ''I can tell you must be a wonderful cook.''

''Yes, I am,'' Grace agreed absently, then she frowned. ''I remember that. I remember that I'm a wonderful cook. But do you know what? Remembering brings conflicting emotions. I can tell I like to cook...even *want* to cook, but there's some sort of negative feeling attached to it, too.''

''You were the only woman on a ranch full of men, Grace,'' Nick said with a laugh. ''Even though you could cook and you could cook well, you probably felt everybody should take a turn, not leave the responsibility to you because you're a woman. If you have any negative feeling attached to cooking, it's not some big, sinister thing. It's just your sense of fair play.''

''Oh, so this was like a woman's-liberation thing with me?''

''Absolutely.''

''That's wonderful,'' Grace said and started to laugh.

''I told you, you didn't let anybody push you around.''

''Maybe you'd better tell me some more about my family before I meet them.''

''Beyond what I've already told you, there isn't much

to tell. Angus is a very wealthy, very quirky venture capitalist who lives on the ranch he also operates. Cal, your biological brother, and Ryan, the other boy Angus raised, were ranch hands. They are good, decent people,'' Nick said, remembering how he used to envy them. Not because they had more than he had, but because they were honest. Direct. Genuine. His entire life had been a lie.

''What do we do now?'' Nick asked, not deliberately changing the subject when Grace removed the frying pan from the stove, but glad to see it shift because even though his past was out in the open, it couldn't be changed and it wasn't a place he cared to visit with regularity.

''Now that everything's sautéed,'' she said, ''we throw all this and some tomatoes into a pot, bring it to a boil and watch it simmer for the next six hours.''

''Now *there's* excitement.''

She tapped his arm in gentle reprimand, but said, ''We'll play rummy while we watch so you're not too bored.''

''Penny a point?'' he suggested, then leaned forward to kiss the tip of her nose.

Grace laughed. ''You're as bad as Stella.''

''I taught Stella.''

Wearing fancy clothes, they ate their spaghetti with wine and candlelight. No one had called, save for Stella, who was checking up on them, but otherwise the day was silent, secluded, and only theirs.

Given Grace's penchant for doing the outrageous, Nick couldn't refuse her when she suggested they dress up as if they were going out for a night on the town...even though they were staying in.

She wore pink chiffon, and pulled her hair into a curly knot, with loose sable tendrils framing her face. Not wanting to be outdone, Nick decided to wear his tuxedo. In a sense, they were creating a fantasy, a memory, and he wasn't going to default on his end of the deal. If they were creating a memory, then by God it would be a good one.

When the last of the spaghetti was gone and the candles had burned to fluorescent nubs, Nick felt a stab of regret so strong he almost couldn't contain himself. He wasn't surprised when Grace rose from her seat and excused herself to go to her room, like Cinderella trying to leave before the stroke of midnight when her coach turned back into a pumpkin.

He let her go because he knew it was the right thing to do. Their life together, this night, had been every bit as much of a fabrication as the one the fairy godmother had created in the fairy tale. Nick understood that by leaving, Grace was subtly telling him that now that she knew they hadn't been living together, his agreement to sleep with her couldn't be honored.

So, he was off the hook. He no longer had to play loving husband and sleep with her. He no longer had to pretend they were in love.

He leaned back in his chair and absorbed the pain of that, knowing this was only the beginning.

Though Grace *had* gone to bed early to let Nick off the hook, it wasn't because she wasn't going to compel him to keep his commitment to sleep with her now that she knew they were separated. She let him off the hook because he seemed so scared, so miserable.

When Grace reached her room, she rummaged through the meager belongings she'd brought home from the hospital until she found Christine Warner's number. Though it was nearly ten, the card Dr. Warner had given her had both the psychiatrist's office and home phone numbers listed, and Grace didn't hesitate to begin dialing. The phone was picked up on the second ring.

"Hello, this is Christine Warner."

"Dr. Warner," Grace said, "this is Grace Spinelli, we met at the hospital in Turner. I'm supposed to see you tomorrow morning."

"Oh, hello, Grace. I'm looking at my book and I can see that you didn't call my secretary and make an appointment. Are you calling now to schedule something?"

Grace bit her bottom lip. "No. Not exactly. Actually, I'm sort of calling for advice."

"What kind of advice?"

"I discovered that my husband and I had been separated."

"Oh."

"Well," Grace admitted guiltily. "Even before I left the hospital, I'd suspected as much."

"But you didn't really remember?"

"No."

"Did being at his house cause you to remember?"

"No, Nick admitted to me that we had been separated. He stayed with me in the hospital and took me in because my family is out of town. When I called the ranch, I discovered my one brother went with my father to Houston and my other brother is on his honeymoon. If Nick would have deserted me, there wouldn't have been anyone else to care for me."

"So, basically, what he did was very generous?"

"Nick is a very sweet, kind and generous person."

"And you really don't want to be separated anymore, do you?" Christine observed shrewdly.

Grace drew a long, uncomfortable breath. "No. But I don't have a clue what to do next."

"Why is it so important to do something?"

"Because my father is scheduled to return on Saturday. When he comes home, I'll be going home, too."

"You're running out of time."

"Yes."

Christine sighed. "I don't know what to tell you, Grace.

Except to suggest that you get your feelings out in the open.''

"I've tried. I've told Nick that no matter what he did to cause our separation, I'd forgive him, but he won't let me forgive him."

"Has he told you what he did?"

This time Grace sighed. "I don't want him to tell me what he did."

"Why not?"

"I have the distinct impression that once he voices this thing, he'll close up. I'd like to know what I'm forgiving him for, but I also recognize that once it's out in the open, Nick won't be able to deal with me anymore."

"Grace, because you don't remember anything, what's happening is almost like a double whammy. Not only did Nick have to deal with the fact that he did something wrong at the time that he did it, but now he has to admit it to you again, face your reaction again and once again live with the consequences. Your reaction and the consequences were bad enough the first time he lost you. It's no wonder he doesn't want to admit it a second time." She paused, and drew a ragged breath. "Frankly, the only thing that could save the two of you right now is for you to get your memory back, remember what he did and go to him with forgiveness so that he doesn't have to see your reaction and so that he doesn't have to face any more consequences."

Grace squeezed her eyes shut. "Thanks for your help, but I'm not having much luck in the memory department."

"Isn't *anything* jogging your memory? Aren't you getting any memories at all? No feelings? No impressions? No insights of any kind?"

"No...yes," Grace said, suddenly remembering that making spaghetti sauce had brought feelings, if nothing else. "Today, while I was cooking, I remembered that I loved to cook, but I also got some negative impressions. Nick told me that was because I was the only woman on my father's ranch and I hated to be relegated to doing all the cooking just because I was a girl."

"In other words, cooking stimulated your memory?"

"Yes," Grace emphatically replied.

"That's probably because the act of cooking is familiar. Though Nick's house isn't familiar, and even his kitchen isn't all that familiar, *cooking* is familiar. It's obviously something that you do regularly and therefore something that will help stimulate your memory."

"You're right."

"Then, Grace, my advice to you is to start cooking."

The next morning, Nick awakened to the scents of coffee and cinnamon. Cautious, he snuck down the stairs and edged his way into the kitchen. Seeing the mess before him, he gasped. "What are you doing?"

Flour was everywhere. Though the large tin canister sat on the butcher block, Grace had managed to drip, drag or drop the white powder to nearly every available surface in the kitchen. Pans sat in haphazard stacks beside their storage cabinet, as if she'd been searching for the right one and had left the others where she set them when she realized they were inappropriate.

"Baking," Grace replied happily. "Nick, it's amazing. It's like I've found myself." She patted her chest with flour-covered hands. "My *real* self."

Of all the possible pictures Nick had conjured of Grace, being a baker wasn't one of them. "Grace, I told you that you like to cook, but you refused to do it all the time because it's not fair to dump all the responsibility onto one person."

"I understand what you're saying," Grace agreed, then began to skillfully roll out dough. When it was flat, she greased it with margarine, then sprinkled sugar and cinnamon across the top before she rolled it into a long cylinder. As she cut the cylinder, Nick recognized she was making cinnamon rolls. "And I know that I don't cook for a living," she told him, "but all this work has been bringing back memories like you wouldn't believe."

Cautious, Nick poured himself a cup of coffee. "Care to tell me any of them?"

"I remember my father," Grace said happily. "Not just Angus, my adoptive father—the father you know—but also my real father. I remember Cal and Ryan." She paused, took a long breath. "I even remember you."

He froze. "You do?"

"Not everything. Not all of it. Most of the memories coming back are more like pictures."

The timer for the stove rang and Grace extracted a batch of cinnamon rolls. Plump and brown, they dripped with bubbling sugar and cinnamon. "Aren't they wonderful?"

"They smell wonderful," Nick slowly agreed.

Seeing his reaction, Grace set the pan on an available countertop and said, "I know you're afraid of me getting my memory back, but you don't have to be afraid anymore. I know we weren't living together. I understand that had a great deal to do with your past. I'm not going to punish you again for something that's over and done."

Again, her generosity humbled him. He wasn't sure what to say...how to react. He cleared his throat and pointed at the warm cinnamon rolls. "Can we eat those?"

Grace laughed. "If you ice them."

"How do you ice them?"

"Well, you take this little bowl of maple frosting that I made," Grace said, grabbing a small spatula and dipping it into the creamy mixture. "And you smear it across the top like this."

"I can handle that."

"I thought you could," Grace said and kissed him

soundly on the mouth. "But let's let them cool a minute, first. Eat this one while you wait," she added, handing him the warm, sticky roll, which she had slathered with the creamy frosting.

The ease with which she kissed him left Nick a little stunned. It almost seemed that the more of her memory Grace got back, the more she loved him. It was amazing. And odd. Very odd considering that he was absolutely positive exactly the opposite would happen.

"Get any other flashbacks?" he asked, sliding onto the stool by the counter to eat his cinnamon roll. He was feeling comfortable with the fact that she was getting memories because *she* was comfortable. Unfortunately, though he wasn't Sigmund Freud, or even Joyce Brothers, he also wasn't so foolish as to become complacent. Above and beyond the truth that Nick had hurt her ten years ago was the very real possibility that someone in her life had made her afraid to return home, and that was why she had been blocking the memories before this. She could be getting her memories back now because she felt so relaxed, happy, and safe here with him.

"Well," Grace began carefully, "I did remember that I was seeing someone…almost."

Nick's heart stopped. He genuinely believed his heart stopped. The pain of realizing not just that this was the "someone" who might have been hurting her, but also that she'd found someone else and might be promised to someone else, caused a physical paralysis in the center of his chest. He had to force himself to breathe.

"I say I was *almost* dating someone," Grace continued as she busied herself with the cinnamon rolls as if talking about this was as difficult for her as it was for him. "Because I clearly remember that I didn't even want to go out on a date until you and I were divorced."

"Oh."

"Yeah, oh."

Knowing that it wasn't any of his business if she wanted to date someone, Nick nonetheless realized he had to probe for the answers to the more pressing question of whether or not this guy hit her, or had done anything to make her afraid to get back her memory.

"What was his name?"

"I don't remember. I don't have all my memory back. Just odd bits and pieces. But I do remember that he was a friend of Angus's. I keep thinking his name was Beauregard, but somehow I know that's not right."

Nick burst out laughing. "Beauregard! That's what Cal used to call *every* guy who tried to date you."

Grace smiled. "Really?"

"Yes. If you're remembering Beauregard, that's probably because that's what Cal called him."

"That's a relief."

"Anything else you remember?"

"Well, the other thing I remember about him is that he's an investment counselor and that he has something to do with my present job... Oh, I own my own business. I do about the same thing you do, except I don't sneak into companies. Shareholders don't come to me. The company itself seeks me out."

Nick lifted his coffee cup and took a long swig. "That doesn't surprise me," he said, remembering that she'd always wanted to go in that direction.

If anything was surprising, it was that Nick had inadvertently followed *her* career path. Also, she seemed to have casually accepted that he'd lied to her about her occupation...or at least her place of employment. Obviously she understood that Nick had felt it a necessary evil to tell her a few things that weren't quite true. But even though those were two positive observations, neither of them helped him to ascertain if the guy she wanted to date hurt her.

"Do you remember anything personal about old Beauregard?"

Grace's face scrunched up as if she were in pain. "Oh, don't call him that. It makes me crazy."

Remembering her reaction from when Cal called *him* Beauregard, Nick smiled and relented. "Okay. Do you remember anything personal about whoever he was you thought you wanted to date?"

"Frankly, I hardly remember anything at all about him, except that I needed a divorce to be able to date him. From the way my memories are running, I'd almost be willing to bet that I'd only known him long enough professionally that I was *beginning* to think I'd like to date him."

Nick sighed heavily. "Grace, this isn't helping me."

"Isn't helping you what?" Grace said, then bent to slide another tray of cinnamon rolls into the oven.

Remembering his own responsibilities, Nick began to put maple icing on the rolls that had now cooled. The task also helped keep him busy while he confronted her with his difficult discussion.

"You told me Dr. Ringer thought you were afraid to go home," he said finally. "Dr. Ringer also asked me some odd questions about our life together, which I realized didn't really relate to me, but to someone in your life now. And I assumed that somebody you knew...someone in your life...hit you, hurt you, abused you somehow. I'm trying to figure out what it was that had you so afraid you didn't want to go home."

Grace bit her bottom lip. "Nick, I wasn't afraid to go home. I sensed all along that you didn't want to take me home. I had guessed that we were separated."

"So, old Beauregard doesn't hit you?"

"I told you, I really don't know him in a personal way. I seem to only know him professionally."

"And there isn't anything at the ranch you're afraid of?"

Grace started to laugh. "Heavens, no! When I think of the ranch, I get a severe case of the warm fuzzies. I have nothing in my life to be afraid of." She paused, drew a breath for courage and added, "Except losing you."

"Grace," Nick said, but he used her name like a caution.

"I know. I know. We're living separate lives now. And you don't think I remember enough of my past to make accurate assumptions, but even though everything at home is wonderful, and even though I'm successful and I have the two most wonderful brothers on the face of the earth..." She paused long enough to catch his gaze. "Even though everything in my life couldn't be better, would you believe I'm lonely?"

"Oh, Grace, you don't know that."

"Yes, I do," Grace emphatically contradicted him. "I don't need a memory to tell me that I'm lonely. I can feel it."

She hadn't had a memory, but she'd had a clear sense— one of those swift flashes of insight—that she hadn't been able to get her life together after Nick left her. Oh, her business had flourished. Her family loved her. But she obviously hadn't had the guts or gumption to get a divorce. She'd lived in limbo for however long they'd been separated, not seeking to actually dissolve their union in spite of the fact that they weren't living together.

And neither had Nick gotten a divorce.

With or without a memory, the reality that neither had even tried for a divorce was a very telling thing.

She'd eased them out of sleeping together the night before because once she discovered they weren't living as husband and wife, she understood why Nick was so nervous around her. It even seemed fraudulent to her to share the same bed without some sort of commitment.

But now that she remembered enough about Nick's leaving her to realize it was the saddest, most difficult thing that had ever happened to her, she knew her first intuition was right on the money.

The commitment was there. But they just weren't ready to admit it.

The one thing they needed more than anything was time...

And the one thing they didn't have was time.

Chapter Fifteen

"That was Stella."

"Uh-oh, that doesn't sound good," Grace said, meeting Nick halfway as he walked out of the den and into the family room.

"It isn't. Now another of her grandkids has the chicken pox. The good news is, her daughter-in-law doesn't work on Saturdays so she can be over on Saturday morning. The bad news is, it won't be Saturday for two days."

Grace laughed. "Come on now. You're not helpless and neither am I. Not only have we kept ourselves fairly well fed over the last two days, but we're not doing too badly in the entertainment department, either."

"I know, but I feel like I'm keeping you captive."

"You're not keeping me captive. We're waiting for word from Angus and Cal about when they will be home so I can go home."

At least that's what she kept telling him. Now that her memory had begun to return, it surprised her that Nick hadn't realized he could send her home without her family being there. But she didn't want to go home any more than she wanted her brother and father to return from Houston more quickly.

Cal and Angus were due back on Saturday morning. So she had two days. Two more precious days. And she was taking them. For two people in the process of trying to put their lives back together again, time was a very precious commodity. Two days was like a gift from heaven.

Everything was going wonderfully. They weren't sleeping together. They weren't necking on the sofa. But they were stealing kisses and having long conversations and spending every minute of every day together.

"Since you're so concerned about Stella being away, what do you say we spend the day doing something Stella would have done?"

He eyed her suspiciously. "Like what?"

"How about laundry?"

"Now *that's* entertainment," Nick said sarcastically, then began to laugh. "Grace, I don't want you to use all your time here as a substitute housekeeper. Why don't we go antiquing like you wanted to the other day?"

"You mean it?"

"Of course I mean it."

"What about the call we're waiting for?"

Nick sighed. "Grace, if we haven't gotten a call by now, we're probably not going to get one. Angus and Cal will be home on Saturday, and, if you don't mind, I'd like to keep you here until then. I know you're better. I know your memory's coming back. But I'd rather that you stay with me."

Grace smiled. Obviously they were on the same wavelength. Their relationship was too precarious for them to admit they were trying to reconcile, but they both knew they were. Otherwise, she would have been long gone by now.

"Okay, so, let's go antiquing."

* * *

"You shouldn't have bought that for me."

"You wanted it."

"I know I *wanted* it," Grace countered, as exasperated with herself as she was with him. She didn't have a clue what she was going to do with the clock he'd bought her, because despite all the picturelike memories she'd gotten of her family, her friends, even her co-workers, she hadn't gotten a clear picture of where she lived. How could she explain that she wanted the damn clock because she thought it would look perfect in their house—his house. She didn't know if it would fit the decor of her house— or apartment, or condo, or town house, or tent—for all she knew, she could live in a tent.

And now she had a clock to take home to remind herself that she'd completely misunderstood everything she'd thought was happening between them the past two days.

Frustrated, she made her way to the family room, where she fell to the fat, floral sofa. She knew it wouldn't do her one bit of good to be angry. She also had no clue why she had lost the wonderful patience that had seen her through the past week alone with him. All she knew was that she was tired, annoyed and semifurious.

She suspected that knowing only fragments of her life had worn down her patience. But she also suspected that she was more frustrated with not really knowing where she stood with Nick. Because the truth was, Nick's gift had thrown her. Not so much the gift, but the way in which he'd purchased it.

Up until the very last second, she'd thought he was buying the clock, not for her, but for *them*—for their house. But after he'd paid for it, he'd handed it to her reverently, and sweetly said, "I hope you enjoy this in your home as much as I've enjoyed being with you."

It took every ounce of control not to gape at him, and

even more control not to throw the damn clock to the ground and jump on it until it was nothing but broken wood and twisting springs.

He was driving her nuts.

Frankly, that was the bottom line. One minute he seemed to love her, adore her, want to be with her, and the next he pulled back as if he almost didn't believe they were getting along, and he wasn't about to tempt fate by committing to her...

That was it. In fact, that was almost what Dr. Warner had told her.

Nick wasn't going back and forth because of indecision about his feelings for her, but because he didn't want to risk getting hurt again.

Reeling in her temper, she scrubbed her hand across her mouth and closed her eyes. No wonder their wires had gotten crossed today. She was treating a symptom, not the real problem.

"Are you ready to start supper?" he asked, stepping into the family room.

Grace drew a long breath. Frustrated and tired, she was tempted to tell him she'd rather cook alone tonight because she didn't care to put up with his mood swings, then realized that Nick might not know what he was doing. He might not realize how many times and how many ways he showed her that he loved her, then took it all back with a careless choice of words. Which meant he also didn't realize that his back-and-forth behavior was driving her crazy.

From her reaction to him this afternoon, he probably thought *she* had mood swings.

She eyed him suspiciously. "Actually, I thought we'd just make stir-fry."

"I like stir-fry," he replied innocently.

"That's good because it'll take both of us to make it.

You know, vegetables to chop, beef to brown, all that stuff.''

"Grace, I'm perfectly capable of chopping a vegetable," Nick said, then took her hand to help her stand.

"Good, then we shouldn't have any problem."

In the kitchen, Grace surreptitiously studied him as he gathered the supplies they needed for dinner. He was calm, happy, actually. His temper was gone. The distance he'd so casually put between them had melted like a late-spring snow.

"I remember I used to cook a lot with my mother," he announced suddenly and Grace slid onto one of the stools by the counter, watching him.

"She would spend so much time fretting about what to make, she'd let too much time go by and she'd end up with only a little left to actually cook something."

"So you'd help her?"

"I'd help her," Nick conceded easily. "It never once crossed my mind that the other guys in school might have thought I was a sissy for knowing how to marinate a steak. If we had a steak, I was just damn glad to have it. It didn't bother me one bit to be the one to have to cook it..."

He had become so comfortable talking about his past with her that Grace knew they had gotten beyond it. They were compatible. They'd spent days alone with limited sources of entertainment and had enjoyed each other's company thoroughly. And she couldn't forget how he'd made love to her, as if he'd been searching for her or waiting for her his entire life. He loved her. She didn't have a doubt in her mind that he loved her. The problem was, even if he knew it, even if he admitted it to himself, he wouldn't do a thing about it because he didn't want to get hurt.

Because he was talking, filling her in on his past as he made their dinner, Grace didn't intrude. She didn't even try to help. When their food was almost done, she unobtrusively rose from her seat by the counter and began to set the table. Through it all, Nick talked and talked. He told her so much, Grace was confused about where the line actually was that marked their married and their separated lives. But one thing was clear. They had been separated for a while. Probably years. She would guess at least two.

"I think you tricked me."

Glancing up as Nick presented her with her dinner, Grace smiled. "How?"

"You got me talking so much, I ended up cooking dinner alone."

"You were doing such a good job, I didn't want to interrupt."

"Likely story. Just for that, you get to do the dishes."

"Let's save the dishes for morning."

"Stella hates a messy kitchen," Nick said then snapped open his napkin.

"Stella won't be here.

"In fact," Grace said, leaning toward him so she could give him a quick kiss, testing his reaction, "we're all alone for the next two days."

Rather than being breathless with passion from her innuendo, he drew in a sharp breath as if concerned. "Does that bother you?"

"No," she said, no longer confused but wondering if *he'd* missed a memo. She'd never refused any sort of romantic attention from him, yet he acted as if she shouldn't want to be alone with him.

He didn't know...or didn't understand...that now that he had come to terms with his past, now that he could talk to her openly, honestly and in abundance, now that he was comfortable with her again, they were actually in the process of reconciling. Whether or not he understood it, whether or not he wanted to be, and whether or not he was afraid of getting his heart broken, he was reconciling with her.

She would have to tell him.

No, maybe what she had to do was show him.

Chapter Sixteen

"Well, I guess I'm going to go and get ready for bed," Grace said, and began to push her chair away from the table.

Nick wasn't sure what to do. Now that Grace knew most of the truth about their relationship, he understood that she wouldn't want any sort of romantic entanglement with him, but it still hurt that she wanted to get away from him so quickly. Just as it had hurt that she didn't want to accept a gift from him. He thought he'd more or less dissolved the uneasiness between them with his non-stop talking through dinner, but given that she was so anxious to leave him, he supposed he hadn't.

Although he didn't want her to go, Nick jumped to his feet to pull her chair away from the table. "So soon?"

"I'm a little tired," Grace admitted. She was standing so close he could have touched her, but he knew better. Not only was their present peace a very strained peace, but this time tomorrow they could get a call from Renee or Angus and everything would be gone but the memories...

Ironic. She'd get her memories back and he'd have nothing but memories for the rest of his life.

"I really wouldn't mind if you'd come in and say good-night, though," she suggested quietly, and caught his gaze with her beautiful violet eyes.

He would have breathed a sigh of relief that she was giving him another few minutes with her, but it hurt too much. These little snatches of time spent together would make wonderful memories, but knowing that she didn't return his feelings, these interludes were nothing but an illusion. And every time he had to leave her, he felt as if he was relinquishing a part of his soul.

Nonetheless, he knew he couldn't resist.

"Okay," he said. "Just yell when you're ready for bed."

Smiling slightly, she shook her head. "No. Just give me fifteen minutes. That's all I'll need."

"All right," Nick agreed, and watched her walk out of the kitchen. She had a grace and style and sense of self like no other woman that he'd known. Mature, self-assured, and yet somehow vulnerable, she'd wormed her way into his heart, into his soul. He watched the door close behind her and wondered how the hell he'd live the rest of his life without her, then reminded himself he could do anything—absolutely anything—he set his mind to.

The only problem was, he didn't *want* to do this. He didn't want to hurt anymore. He wanted everything he'd thrown away ten years before.

Nick passed his fifteen minutes by slipping out of his jeans and sweater, showering and putting on his pajama bottoms and robe. Because he didn't think he'd be sleeping tonight, he went to his study and searched for a good book, something he'd already read so it would feel like an old friend, then he began the slow walk to Grace's room.

When he opened the bedroom door, he discovered the

lights were out and the bathroom door was open. The scent of lilacs and the pale illumination of candlelight led him to the bathroom.

"Grace?"

"In here," she whispered. He followed the sound of her voice only to discover she was sitting in the oversize beige oval tub up to her neck in bubbles.

He cleared his throat, but couldn't quite force himself to walk away from her. "I thought you said you'd be ready for a good-night kiss in fifteen minutes?"

She smiled. "I am." She sunk a little deeper beneath the bubbles. "Kiss me."

Not quite sure if she'd decided to extend her scented bath and wanted him to kiss her and leave her to her warm bubbles, or if she was teasing him, Nick stood helplessly.

"Don't you want to kiss me good-night?" she asked throatily.

"Yes," Nick whispered back, becoming mesmerized. The scent, the candlelight, the seductive woman immersed in bubbles all worked together to make him forget everything. If asked, he'd be hard-pressed to remember his first, middle and last names.

"Then come here."

He decided to kiss her and get the hell out. He set his book on an available table and took the three steps to the tub. Bending, he brushed his lips across hers, but her hands burst from beneath the pearlescent mounds and she caught the lapel of his robe. Staring into his eyes, she pressed her lips to his, rubbing them seductively, then parting them and sliding her tongue into his mouth.

She never released his gaze. Instead, as she kissed him, she rose, maneuvering him into a standing position as she pushed herself out of the water. Naked, dripping with bubbles, she stepped into his waiting arms.

Feeling the last vestiges of sanity deserting him, Nick

murmured, "Grace, stop. We shouldn't be doing this. I've told you, we're not living together."

Lips pressed against his mouth, she said, "I know."

"So, we shouldn't be doing this."

"Nick," she said, her voice nearly exasperated. "We've been reconciling since the day you came to rescue me in the hospital."

That stopped him. He pushed away from her. "Reconciling?" he asked softly.

"You know, when two people who think they want to get a divorce decide they really don't want a divorce after all?"

"You don't mean that."

She laughed. "Of course I mean it. Nick, look at us. I started getting my memory back two days ago. I could have left here anytime since then, but I *chose* not to. And you asked me to stay. Do you know why?"

He licked his dry lips.

"Because we love each other," she said.

"Yes, we do," Nick agreed, and began kissing her cheeks. If this was a mirage, he was taking it. If this was a miracle, he needed it. In a sense, he finally understood he'd been waiting to be able to deal with his past so that he could go to her, but now he saw that he couldn't deal with his past without her. He couldn't do anything important without her. He *needed* her. He wanted her. He loved her. "We really do."

She pulled away from him. Caught his gaze. "Then show me. Take me to bed."

The candlelight from the bathroom didn't reach the bedroom. Instead, they relied on the moonlight spilling in through the uncurtained French doors. Sleek and warm, her skin skimmed over his as they tumbled to the bed. He easily lost his loose robe and pajama bottoms, and, when he was completely naked and pressed against her, Nick drew a long breath and simply savored the satin of her flesh against his.

Balancing himself on his elbows, he bent down to kiss her willing mouth, and as they kissed, her arms came around him and their legs entwined. Because they had been inexperienced, impatient teenagers the first time they made love, and because the second time had been filled with desperation, Nick vowed that he would not only take his time, he would relish every second of this opportunity.

He kissed every inch of her body. He stroked, caressed, teased and nibbled his way from the crown of her head to the soles of her feet. One minute, Grace felt weak with bone-melting arousal, the next she shivered with need. The house was silent, save for an occasional rustle of the wind through the trees and their breathless sighs.

When she realized Nick was making up for everything that had passed between them, Grace pressed her palm to his chest and tumbled him to his back and returned the favor, kissing him, nibbling sensitive skin and caressing every nook and cranny and crevice, until without warning he grabbed her shoulders and swung her around. Kissing her fiercely, he rolled her to her back and completed their union.

His intensity of feeling was nearly frightening, but Grace was strong enough to handle it. She met him thrust for thrust, need for need, until in a burst of emotion they both found fulfillment, and, at long last, love.

When sanity finally returned, Nick reached over and pulled Grace to him. He felt whole, and loved, and somehow powerful. As if he could take on the world and win.

"I can't believe you're willing to try again."

"Oh, Nick," Grace said, then sleepily snuggled against him. "Of course I want to try again. I don't think I've really wanted anything else."

"I wanted a lot of other things in life, Grace. It was

important for me to become successful. I couldn't really stand to be poor anymore..."

She nodded, realizing that had probably been part of what broke them apart. She was accustomed to comfort, maybe even to the point that she took it for granted.

"I understand that. For every bit as much as it was important for me not to rely on Angus's money, influence and power," she said, "it was important for you to succeed."

Happy, damn near euphoric, he hugged her to him. "I'm never going to let you get away again."

"I don't want to go anywhere but to sleep," Grace said, snuggling against him some more.

Kissing the top of her head, Nick recognized that not only was she drifting off to dreamland, she deserved to be. They'd had a long day, and she was still in the final stages of her recuperation. He shouldn't have kept her up so long.

"I'm sorry," he said. "I know you're tired. I should have let you get to sleep sooner."

"Nick, we just agreed to reconcile," she said sleepily. "I think that's worth losing a few hours' sleep over." He felt her smile against his chest. "In fact, I'd do it again."

He kissed the crown of her head. "Don't tempt me."

"Oh, I'll have plenty of time to tempt you and I plan to tempt you. Just not tonight. I'm not letting another year or two years go by without having you in my life."

Content, Nick settled down to go to sleep himself, but in the last seconds before he, too, would have drifted off, he realized what Grace had said. *She wasn't letting another year or two go by without having him in her life?* Did she mean that she didn't want to waste another minute, let alone another year, or did she think they'd only been separated a year or two?

"Grace?" he whispered, trying to get her attention if

she was awake, but also trying not to wake her if she'd already fallen asleep. "Grace?"

When she didn't answer, Nick knew she was asleep. An odd, uncomfortable feeling settled in the pit of his stomach. The more he thought about her last comment, the more he realized she thought they'd only been separated a year or two.

Damn it! Squeezing his eyes shut, Nick swore softly under his breath. With the way she'd been having memories that day, Nick didn't really have a clue how much of her life she actually remembered, but from the things she'd said, he'd assumed she remembered much, much more than just the basics. Especially when she got angry with him in the antique store. That's why he'd talked so much while making dinner. He'd wanted her to see that he'd spent ten dry, lonely years.

Damn it! He thought she knew.

Drawing in a long, deep breath, Nick pulled her more tightly against him and knew he was going to have to tell her everything in the morning. As difficult as it was going to be, he was going to have to tell her the whole story, line by line, until she understood exactly what had happened between them. Then, after the whole truth was on the table, he'd ask her if she still felt the same way about the reconciliation.

Part of him believed she would.

The other part wasn't even half that optimistic.

Nick was awakened by the loud blare of a car horn. He bounced up in bed, but Grace slid her head under the pillow. "Hey, there is nowhere to run and nowhere to hide," he said, lightly slapping her backside. "Obviously, whoever is down there wants our attention."

Even as he said the last, Nick realized who it was. Angus. Renee must have reached Angus. No one else would be so bold, or so impatient, that they'd toot a car horn at five-thirty in the morning.

Nick froze. What he needed right now was another day with Grace. A few hours to explain their past to her. A few hours for her to think about it. A few hours for him to beg her forgiveness and to convince her the reconciliation was the right thing to do.

The horn blared again.

"Oh, for Pete's sake," Grace grumbled and rolled out of bed. Nick tried to grab her hand to stop her, but his fingers brushed her wrist without grasping it. She walked to the small window, and as she looked outside, Nick watched her stagger as if she'd been hit.

"Oh my God," she whispered. "It's Angus and Cal. And there's another car...a police car right behind them... Ryan! Oh my God, it's Ryan... And Madison. His new wife, Madison. Ryan had just gotten married the day before I... Oh my God."

A torrent of memories overwhelmed Grace, making her feel as if she was going to faint. Unlike the simple, friendly pictures she'd been getting the day before, these memories came complete with emotions. Overpowering love. The joy of friendship. The pain of separation. And the pain of betrayal.

She fell to the bed and Nick caught her shoulders. "Grace?" he whispered hoarsely. "Grace, you have to listen to me. I have some important things I need to tell you—"

"Like we *never* lived together as husband and wife?" she interrupted angrily. "Like we haven't even *seen* each other in ten years?" Furious, she spun around in his arms. "What was this, some kind of joke to you? Damn it, Nick, we're virtual strangers and you led me to believe we were...lovers."

Before he could say a word, she pushed out of his arms and began snatching clothes out of the drawers. "Whose clothes are these?'' she demanded, even though she stepped into them.

Nick didn't answer. Angus's horn blew again.

Hot and furious, the memories licked at her like the flames of a fire. The humiliation of being left the day after the ceremony. The pain of being alone. The ache of waiting, praying that he'd return.

''Just when did you plan on filling me in on all of this?''

He glanced at her. ''This morning.''

''Huh! Likely story,'' she said, then stormed out the door.

Chapter Seventeen

"Grace! Gracie!" Angus called as Grace virtually flew out of Nick's house. Luckily, everyone was racing to see her and misinterpreted her bursting out of the front door as her excitement to see them.

When she reached the bottom step of the front porch, Angus caught her in his arms. "Oh, my great glory, girl! I'm so sorry. Renee told me your accident was the very same day we left and you'd lost your memory."

"I'm fine," Grace said. "Really, it couldn't be helped. Let's just go."

But Angus didn't seem to hear her. Grasping her shoulders, he pushed her away from him so that he could examine her. "I don't see any sign of any lasting injuries."

No, only another broken heart. Another round of humiliation. Another passel of years spent trying to get over a man who did nothing but lie to her.

"I told you, I'm fine."

"She *is* fine," Nick assured everyone as he walked across the front porch. He'd never seen such a collection of dedicated and devoted family members. Cal and Angus he easily recognized. But Ryan Kelly not only looked older and more mature, he finally seemed happy. Nick more than suspected the responsibility for that went to the beautiful woman with whom Ryan currently held hands.

Instead of feeling the stab of jealousy Nick typically experienced when he saw Grace's family, he felt only grateful that she'd have people to confide in, people who would help her cope, and even get through the next few weeks. Because he hadn't meant to hurt her. He'd thought she knew.

"I can't believe it," Angus went on, releasing Grace to Cal and Ryan, both of whom wanted a hug and an opportunity to examine her. "I'm so grateful to you, boy," he said to Nick as he began climbing the steps of Nick's porch. "Fate was smiling on us when Grace not only had an accident near the home of someone she knew, but also when you somehow found out about it."

Nick cleared his throat and decided it wasn't his place to fill Angus in on details. He'd let Grace tell what she wanted to tell in her own way and in her own time. "Turner's a small town, Angus," Nick said, accepting Angus's handshake. "Once I heard about Grace's accident, I couldn't simply leave her alone."

"Well, we're grateful. Damn, damn grateful," Angus said, and Nick knew the old man just barely kept himself from giving Nick one of his famous hugs.

But all Grace wanted was to leave. The overwhelming wash of memories had left her shaking and weak, but recognizing Nick's lies and duplicity was actually making her ill.

Seeing her obvious distress, Cal came up behind her and pulled her away from Madison and Ryan, who were fussing over her. "Are you okay?" he whispered.

She shook her head once, quickly. "No. Damn it, Cal, he led me to believe we'd lived together in an actual mar-

riage, but were separated for a short while. I spent the
past two weeks trying to win him back.''

''I'm going to deck him,'' Cal said as he started to pull
away from her.

Grace stopped him. ''No. Just get me out of here.''

With a speed that not only surprised Grace, but left her
dizzy, too, Cal orchestrated their getaway. First, he shifted
Grace into Ryan's care. ''Put her in Angus's Bronco and
let's get going,'' he said, then walked up the steps of
Nick's front porch.

''Come on, Angus, Grace wants to go home.''

''What... What?'' Angus said, confused. Turning away
from Nick and facing Cal, he added, ''We just got here.
I want to thank...''

''I'm sure Nick doesn't want *thanks* for what he did,''
Cal said, looking Nick square in the eye. In that moment,
Nick felt the weight of the world's injustice as if it were
all his to bear. What he'd done he'd done to try to protect
Grace. But there was no way in hell he could explain that
to these people. Still, in one respect, Cal was right. He
didn't want thanks.

He met Cal's gaze. ''You're right. I don't want thanks.
I felt I owed it to Grace to take care of her and I did.
Now, if you'll excuse me,'' he said, and turned toward
his open front door. ''I have some business to take care
of myself.''

Inside his house, he listened to the rumbles and mur-
murings as the entire MacFarland clan entered their re-
spective vehicles. He snuck to the dining-room window
and pulled the curtain back only far enough that he could
look out, but not so far that anyone could see him. Angus
was in the passenger side of the front seat of his Bronco
and Cal drove. Grace had taken the back seat. She'd rested
her head against the back of the seat as if she was in
complete shock.

Fate.

He hated it.
He absolutely hated it.

"All right," Angus grumbled when they were back on the road again without so much as a cup of coffee or a decent conversation with the man who had cared for Grace. "I want to know what the hell is going on here."

"Nothing, Angus," Cal said. "Grace is tired and she wanted—"

"Baloney," Angus said, turning in his seat so he could look at Grace. "I know when I'm getting the runaround and I'm getting the runaround now. You're not tired, are you, Grace?" He peered at her face. "You're something, but it's not tired. It's not sick, either," he added after studying her. "In fact, if I were to guess, I'd say you were either very, very mad—so angry you're weak from it—or you're not as well recovered from your injuries as you wanted everyone to believe." He studied her closely again. "Are you still hurting?"

"Not hurting," Cal said. "Just tired..."

"Caleb Wright," Angus said, his voice a warning, "let your sister talk for herself."

"He's right, Cal, I can speak for myself," Grace said quietly, then drew a long breath. "The reason Nick was called about my accident was because I had our marriage certificate on the front seat of my car when I wrecked it."

"Your *what?*"

"My marriage certificate," she repeated. "When we were eighteen, Nick and I ran away and got married. When we returned home to tell you what we had done, to get our belongings and to start out for California, we discovered you'd had a heart attack."

Angus scrubbed his hand over his mouth. "Stop the car."

Cal gave Angus a sideways look. "Angus, I can listen and drive—"

"No, I want this story free of distractions." He caught Cal's gaze. "I also want to hear your part in things."

"Cal had no part in things," Grace assured Angus, but Cal pulled the Bronco off to the side of the road anyway.

"The day of Ryan and Madison's wedding," she went on, "I told Cal I was going to Turner to find Nick so that he and I could get a divorce together. I thought it would simplify matters for both of us to be present to sign whatever needed signing and to get everything done and out of the way. But I ran into a storm, and ten minutes before I would have reached Nick's house, I wrecked my car."

By this time, Angus had angled himself on the seat so that he could see both Cal and Grace. "You say you and Nick never saw one another in ten years?"

"No. I spent my first semester at UCLA as I had intended, but when Nick never registered and I couldn't find him anywhere on campus, I transferred to a college closer to home."

Angus cleared his throat. "You told me you'd done that because you needed to be with your family."

"Because I did *need* to be with my family." Grace paused, drew another deep breath and added, "The person I loved more than anything else in this world had deserted me. I *needed* to be close to my family."

Angus scratched his head. "This is very confusing."

Grace laughed slightly because she knew that if she didn't laugh, she'd cry. "You think you're confused? You should be me. All this happened ten years ago, but while I was sick, Nick led me to believe it had all happened a few months ago, a year at most. I know he did it because he was trying to make things easier on me while you were in Houston, but it had the opposite effect. Thinking that we'd only been separated a short while, I tried to put puzzle pieces together that didn't fit, and ended up making assumptions that were all wrong."

"So, you didn't get your divorce while you were there?" Angus asked cautiously.

Grace shook her head and realized that through all this, Cal hadn't said a word. He simply stared out the window. "No," Grace quietly reported. "Actually, because I was so confused, I kept trying to convince Nick that we should reconcile."

"Do you want to reconcile?" Angus asked softly.

Grace shook her head emphatically. "Angus, I haven't seen the man in ten years. The only things I knew about him were things he told me himself..." *And the ways he behaved, the things he did, the very wonderful way he treated her,* Grace admitted, if only to herself.

"No matter how much I loved Nick Spinelli when I was eighteen," she said, "I haven't seen him in ten years. I not only don't love him anymore, I don't know him and I *don't* want to reconcile."

"Which means you're going to have to see him again," Angus advised carefully. "To get your divorce. Are you prepared for that?"

Grace bit her bottom lip. She couldn't see him again. She didn't want to be anywhere near Nick Spinelli. He'd lied to her and he'd made a fool of her. For at least two days, he'd known she'd been desperately trying to reconcile with him, and instead of telling her the truth, he'd slept with her again.

Answering Angus's question, she said, "I may not have to see him if your lawyer handles the divorce for me."

"We'll call Sherron when we get home," Angus said softly as Cal started the Bronco.

But though everything had worked out much, much better than Grace thought it would or could, she got an odd feeling in the pit of her stomach and she looked behind her, up toward the wooded mountain that hid Nick's home.

He was alone again.

It shouldn't have bothered her.

She shouldn't have cared.

But she did.

She reminded herself one more time that he'd not only lied to her, he'd taken the lie as far as it would go, and in doing that, he'd broken her heart…again.

This time when Cal put the Bronco on the road, Grace didn't look back and she vowed she never would.

Chapter Eighteen

"Cal thinks you need someone to talk to."

Grace glanced up at Ryan's wife, Madison. As if sensing she needed added assurance that Grace wouldn't chase her away, Madison held her eighteen-month-old daughter, Lacy, her child from a relationship she had before she met Ryan. Both mother and daughter had blond hair, blue eyes and the face of an angel.

Grace put her hands out to take Lacy. "I'll hold the baby and I'll listen to honeymoon stories, but I don't have anything I need—or want—to talk about."

"Well, Angus still feels like hell that he was away in your hour of need..."

"And I explained that I'd more or less planned it that way," Grace said, then paused to sigh. "Madison, if you look at this from my vantage point, I sort of painted myself into that spot. I didn't want to admit that I'd been married at eighteen. I mean, I wouldn't have cared if things would have ended differently, but for Pete's sake, the guy deserted me the day after he married me. I felt foolish and stupid. And I wanted to handle this in the most private way possible. Your honeymoon and Angus's trip to Houston gave me the perfect opportunity to straighten out my past, so I took it. It isn't Angus's fault, or your fault or Cal's fault that you weren't available. It's all mine."

"Yeah, but we all still feel guilty."

"Well, you shouldn't. Right, Lacy?" Grace said, and bounced Madison's daughter on her knee.

Madison laid her fingers on Grace's forearm. "Grace, how can we not feel guilty? Obviously you didn't feel close enough to any one of us to confide your biggest heartache. You didn't seem to believe in any one of us enough, or trust any one of us enough, to let us help you or share your pain."

"Madison, it all happened ten years ago—"

"I know you thought you were divorced," Madison interrupted. "But Ryan told me that, looking back, it's obvious that you never really dated anyone in ten years. You always made studying, and then creating your business, your top priority, and no one ever paid any attention to the fact that outside of those activities you didn't have much of a life."

"I had exactly the life I wanted."

"Really?" Madison said, and again laid her fingertips on Grace's forearm.

Settling Lacy on her lap, Grace sighed. "Oh, Madison, I didn't mean for ten years to pass. I just didn't want to get hurt again."

"But you did anyway."

"Yeah," Grace admitted softly. She did get hurt, except this time the pain was deeper, stronger, because she knew Nick loved her. The first time around she was never really sure, but this time he'd said it and he meant it. Unfortunately, just like the first time, he simply didn't trust her love enough to give her the truth. He'd much rather let her go, than lay everything on the line and trust that her love was strong enough to accept him as he was. "With or without my memory, I think it would have hurt me to see him again."

"Part of you still loves him," Madison speculated.

"Oh, yeah," Grace said. "I think part of me will always be eighteen and head over heels in love with him."

"But not enough that you would want to give it a second try?"

Grace shook her head. How could she explain to Madison that it wasn't her choice. It was Nick's choice and that's why it hurt so much. She knew that she was the one to leave him this time around, but he never tried to stop her. Once Grace got over her shock and anger, she realized he never even seemed surprised that she was going. He simply shook hands with Angus and went back into his house, almost as if he'd always known the end was coming and he was prepared for it.

Knowing she couldn't really explain this to Madison, Grace shrugged her shoulders and gave the pat answer that made the most sense under the circumstances. "I'm different. He's different." She paused, sighed. "Besides, he lied to me."

"You told Angus this morning that Nick was trying to protect you when he led you to believe you had a normal marriage."

"I told Angus that because I was trying to protect Angus. The truth is, Nick's withholding the truth didn't protect me. It only got me hurt worse. Because he led me to believe we hadn't been separated very long and because I could sense that I loved him, I kept trying to get us to reconcile."

"I still don't see anything wrong with that."

"Yeah, well, I think he should have told me that we hadn't seen each other in ten years before he slept with me." Without giving Madison a chance to answer that, Grace handed Lacy to her, then rose.

"This isn't about feeling foolish, though I feel foolish. It isn't about feeling betrayed, though I feel betrayed. It's more about the fact that he hid his whole life from me," Grace said, for the first time admitting the real truth out loud. "Even while we were dating in high school, I had no idea of how he lived, or who he really was. The real bottom line is that he didn't trust me enough with his life—or his love—to be honest. Unless or until he could be honest with me, we won't have a snowball's chance in hell. And since he couldn't be honest with me after I poured my heart out and virtually begged him to love me, I'd say the odds are pretty good that he's not ever going to be able to trust me."

She walked into the house and up the steps without stopping to say good-night to anyone, and decided that it was time to finish what she'd started.

Tomorrow morning she would call Angus's lawyers, the ones who got paid very well for being deadly and discreet, and she would get exactly what she'd started out to get when this whole mess began.

She would get her divorce and she would get her life back. All of her life. Not just bits and pieces, but all of it.

"So, you're just going to let her go?" Stella asked Nick two weeks later as she marched into his living room. He sat at the piano, the fingers of his right hand dangling across the keys, occasionally making a sound that could pass for music but really wasn't.

"What, exactly, do you think I should do?" Nick countered, waving the legal document he'd received that day. "The lawyers even went so far as to attach a little restraining order on the side. I'd say she means business. I'd say she wants left alone."

"I'd say she's angry because you lied to her," Stella retorted.

"I didn't lie to he

"No, but you didr
because you didn't tr
said is up for interpr
love her, she wouldr
half the things you
guesses."

"Yeah, well, it's a

"Of course it is,"
you're too damn sca
let her heart be brok

"Her heart's not b

"Oh, no," Stella _____ ____ _____ __ __ _____ like the
most devoted, most wonderful husband on the face of the
earth, then let her go without so much as an argument. I
can see that her heart wouldn't be broken. Any woman
would accept that. Don't worry about the fact that she
was sick or vulnerable. I'm sure she'll bounce right
back."

"She has a good family. They'll take care of her."

"And you have no one," Stella said, for the first time
without a hint of sarcasm. "You were different...you
were *happy* with her. And she was very happy with you.
Yet, you'd let her go without a second thought. Are you
that scared? Does your father still control you that
much?"

"You don't know anything about my father."

"What do you think I am, stupid or blind? Every time
your mother comes to visit and she starts talking about
Jake this and Jake that, you turn into a little brick wall. I
might not have met your father personally, but I met him
in various and sundry ways over the past few years, and
I'd say right now he's still got you by the big toe. You
let Grace go, he wins again."

"You wanted to see me, Angus?"
"I inadvertently intercepted a call from *our* lawyer this

morning."
"Oh?" Grace said
gundy chairs in fro
have to say?"
"She said
Nick's si
added
tape

, settling into one of the two bur-
nt of Angus's desk. "What did Sherron

your papers were served and they received
gned copy in return mail. She said," Angus
oftly, "that the rest is nothing but a bunch of red
and to tell you you're very close to being a free
oman."

The pain of that hit Grace like a physical slap and she
felt as if she was going to cry. After two weeks to think
about everything that had happened, a consultation with
Dr. Ringer and a consultation with Christine Warner,
Grace realized two important things. First, Nick had honestly done the best he could do, the right thing given that
Dr. Ringer had warned him a hundred times not to say or
do anything that would upset her. Second, she still loved
him. Always had, always would. And with the swift return
of the signed divorce papers, Grace realized something
else. He wasn't coming after her. He really didn't trust
that anybody could love him. Not even her.

Before she would humiliate herself in front of Angus
by crying over a man she was supposed to hate, Grace
said, "That's good," and began to rise so she could leave
the room.

"Not so fast," Angus said, waving her back down
again. "I had a chance to think about all this stuff, about
everything that happened ten years ago when I had my
heart attack, and all the things that happened when you
went away to school and then came home, and I'm not
happy with how this turned out."

"I wasn't really happy with it, either, Angus," Grace
said, just barely keeping her voice from breaking as she
spoke. "But it's over and done, and as Sherron said, the

papers have not only been served, they got Nick's signed copies in return mail.''

''I want to know what happened.''

Grace cleared her throat. ''Angus, I love you dearly, but this really isn't any of your business.''

''The hell it isn't. Grace,'' he said, softening his tone. ''I spent the last two weeks realizing I must have been a miserable excuse for a father if I didn't catch on to the fact that you'd not only been married but the wretched bastard broke your heart.''

''It's all in the past—''

''No,'' Angus interrupted. ''It's all in the present again. I looked that man in the eye the day we picked you up and I saw something. He cares for you. He was grief-stricken to see you go and you're heartbroken without him. Yet, you called a lawyer and filed papers as if nothing happened.''

Grace sighed. ''Nothing did happen.''

''No,'' Angus contradicted. ''You're wrong. Something did happen. You got the chance to see him again, without any prejudicial feelings about what happened ten years ago. He got the chance to make amends, or at least try. I think from the way you've been behaving since we got home, acting nervous like you've got unfinished business, that you were on your way to straightening out the past, but didn't quite get there. I think,'' Angus said, rising from his chair to stand in front of his desk and face her directly, ''that Cal and I arrived a couple days too soon.''

Grace shook her head. ''Even if we loved one another to distraction, it doesn't matter,'' she said, giving Angus the excuse that kept her strong enough to stay away from Nick. ''He lied to me...''

''No,'' Angus said. ''From what you told Madison the other night, it sounds more like he didn't get around to telling you the whole truth yet.'' He paused, took her hands. ''Gracie, you didn't even try to get serious with another man for ten years. That should tell you something.''

"Angus, what it tells me, and what it should tell you is that I was busy—"

"Gracie," Angus entreated, capturing Grace's fingers in his. "Don't let somebody you love get away."

Grace bit her bottom lip, and she couldn't stop the tears that had been threatening. "He doesn't want me, Angus," she whispered. "He let me go without a fight or an explanation. He never called when he got the divorce papers. He didn't even think about it before signing. He doesn't care. He doesn't want me. He'd rather be alone."

Chapter Nineteen

The next morning, Grace decided she couldn't take another day of Angus's kindness or Cal's moodiness and realized it was her own fault that she was in this position. By staying with them at the ranch, she was giving them the opportunity to feel sorry for her because she was around too much. She had her own apartment in Crossroads Creek and in spite of the fact that she didn't really feel like being alone, it was time to go home.

After breakfast, she packed her belongings and stacked them in her new car, but before she could leave, she wanted one more look around.

Striding past the outbuildings, she made her way to the corral and hooked her booted foot on the lower level of the wooden fence. She watched the sky, the trees and even the dry Texas dirt, and listened to the sounds of silence, realizing that this was her heritage.

She'd lived alone for so long, basically kept even her close family an arm's distance away for so long, that she would either have to spend the rest of her life very much alone, or once she recovered from the pain of losing Nick again, she'd have to do some hard and diligent work to get close to her family.

Unfortunately, she wasn't sure she'd ever get over the pain of losing Nick a second time, which meant she wasn't sure if or when she'd ever be able to make amends to her family.

"Hi."

It took only one word for Grace to know Nick was behind her. But because she was so desperate to see him again, Grace thought she was hearing things. For a good thirty seconds, she didn't move, didn't breathe, positive she'd turned the music of the wind into a daydream.

"I said hi."

Even as the sound of Nick's voice moved along her skin like a warm breeze, it sent shivers down her spine. He could hurt her again if she let him, because she wanted very much to hear him say that he needed her, loved her, wanted her. She wanted it so much she had to hold herself back from jumping into his arms. But unless he came not just ready to make a commitment, but knowing how to make a commitment, she couldn't take him back.

Slowly, cautiously, she turned to face him. "What do you want?"

He cleared his throat. "Actually, I have two things for you. One," he said, holding up the paper she recognized as the divorce documents Angus's lawyer had drawn up for her, "is the signed copy of the divorce papers you sent me."

"My lawyer told me she already had those."

"Well, she did," Nick admitted. "But I have a friend, who has a friend, who has a friend, who could get it back for me. I didn't ask how and he didn't tell me."

"Oh, in other words, you had someone break into my lawyer's office and—"

"I don't know and I don't care," Nick said, silencing her. "I wanted the papers back because I wanted the chance to hand them to you personally. I want to give you the choice. You can have this,'' he said, shaking the paper once. ''Or you can have this,'' he added, digging with his free hand into the right front pocket of his jeans. When he brought his hand out, he extended it palm up, revealing an unpretentious gold wedding band, a band exactly like the one he'd given her ten years ago.

She looked at him.

''It's your choice,'' he explained slowly. ''I'll give you the divorce if that's what you really want. But this is what I want,'' he said, indicating the wedding ring. ''I want another chance.''

She remembered the hurt, the confusion, the frustration, and wasn't sure she could go through that again. If he didn't realize yet that a commitment meant that you trusted the person you loved with even the most minute details of your life, then the truth was, he would only hurt her again. ''I don't know.''

''Oh, Grace, don't do this to me. Don't leave me. I know I don't deserve a second chance. I don't even deserve your forgiveness, but I don't want to live without you. I've never known anyone I care about like I care about you. You're the first person I've ever really talked to. I never knew how to be honest. It sort of makes me scared now to try, but it scares me more to know that the alternative to being honest is that I have to live without you.''

Looking at him, with the sun glistening off his shiny black hair and seeing the sincerity in his eyes, Grace remembered so many things, like sitting on their bed eating muffins and laughing about the fact that he'd eaten apple butter for three months straight because his father couldn't hold down a job.

She remembered how he'd thought to bring her clothes and clean pajamas every day in the hospital and that he hadn't hesitated to buy her breakfast, lunch and dinner.

She remembered the pain she saw in his eyes every time she wanted him to kiss her, and she knew, she absolutely knew that not only had he suffered enough, but he loved her.

"I'll take the ring on one condition," she said, then snatched it from his fingers before he had a chance to change his mind.

"What's the condition?"

"That we make spaghetti sauce," she said, then started toward the house as if accepting a wedding ring so perfunctorily was a perfectly normal thing to do.

"Spaghetti sauce?" he said, scrambling after her.

"Yeah, I found a recipe for this really great stuff, but this time you add a pork chop."

"You're kidding."

"No, you really do. You add a pork chop."

He grabbed her bicep and spun her around. "Grace, stop. You're driving me crazy. You've got to have a better condition than spaghetti sauce."

"No, I don't," she said, then rose on tiptoe to kiss his lips. "I love you. I always have loved you. I always will love you. I don't want to beat the past to death. Don't even really want to hear too much about it anymore because it's time for us to move into the future. And for us, the future is spaghetti sauce. Simple chores."

"Simple chores are soothing chores."

She smiled at him. "No. Simple chores are happy chores. Simple chores are the things that people do for each other because they love each other. That's real life. That's normal life. That's what we both want."

He bent to kiss her and Grace stretched to meet him, her heart singing. It might have taken him ten years to come to terms with his past, but he had, and together they'd have everything they'd ever wanted.

Simple chores.
Happy chores.
And maybe even a baby or two.

* * * * *

Beloved author *Judy Christenberry*
brings us an exciting new miniseries in

LUCKY CHARM SISTERS

Meet Kate in January 1999 in
MARRY ME, KATE (SR #1344)
He needed to avoid others meddling in his life. *She*
needed money to rebuild her father's dream. So William
Hardison and Kate O'Connor struck a bargain....

Join Maggie in February 1999 in
BABY IN HER ARMS (SR #1350)
Once Josh McKinney found his infant girl, he needed a
baby expert—quickly! But the more time Josh spent with
her, the more he wanted to make Maggie O'Connor his
real wife....

Don't miss Susan in March 1999 in
A RING FOR CINDERELLA (SR #1356)
The last thing Susan Greenwood expected was a marriage proposal! But cowboy Zack Lowery needed a
fiancée to fulfill his grandfather's dying wish....

A boss, a brain and a beauty. Three sisters marry for
convenience...but will they find love?

THE LUCKY CHARM SISTERS only from

Silhouette®

Available wherever Silhouette books are sold.

Take 2 bestselling love stories FREE

Plus get a FREE surprise gift!

Special Limited-Time Offer

Mail to Silhouette Reader Service™

3010 Walden Avenue
P.O. Box 1867
Buffalo, N.Y. 14240-1867

YES! Please send me 2 free Silhouette Romance™ novels and my free surprise gift. Then send me 6 brand-new novels every month, which I will receive months before they appear in bookstores. Bill me at the low price of $2.90 each plus 25¢ delivery and applicable sales tax, if any.* That's the complete price, and a saving of over 10% off the cover prices—quite a bargain! I understand that accepting the books and gift places me under no obligation ever to buy any books. I can always return a shipment and cancel at any time. Even if I never buy another book from Silhouette, the 2 free books and the surprise gift are mine to keep forever.

215 SEN CH7S

Name	(PLEASE PRINT)	
Address	Apt. No.	
City	State	Zip

This offer is limited to one order per household and not valid to present Silhouette Romance™ subscribers. *Terms and prices are subject to change without notice. Sales tax applicable in N.Y.

USROM-98

©1990 Harlequin Enterprises Limited

FOLLOW THAT BABY...

*the fabulous cross-line series featuring the
infamously wealthy Wentworth
family...continues with:*

THE MILLIONAIRE AND
THE PREGNANT PAUPER
by Christie Ridgway
(Yours Truly, 1/99)

When a very expectant mom-to-be from
Sabrina Jensen's Lamaze class visits the Wentworth
estate with information about the missing heir, her baby
is delivered by the youngest millionaire Wentworth,
who proposes a marriage of convenience....

Available at your favorite retail outlet, only from

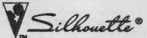

For a limited time, Harlequin and Silhouette have an offer you just can't refuse.

In November and December 1998:

BUY **ANY** TWO HARLEQUIN
OR SILHOUETTE BOOKS and
SAVE $10.00
off future purchases

OR BUY ANY THREE HARLEQUIN OR SILHOUETTE BOOKS
AND **SAVE $20.00** OFF FUTURE PURCHASES!

(each coupon is good for $1.00 off the purchase of two
Harlequin or Silhouette books)

••

JUST BUY 2 HARLEQUIN OR SILHOUETTE BOOKS, SEND US YOUR
NAME, ADDRESS AND 2 PROOFS OF PURCHASE (CASH REGISTER
RECEIPTS) AND HARLEQUIN WILL SEND YOU A COUPON BOOKLET
WORTH $10.00 OFF FUTURE PURCHASES OF HARLEQUIN OR
SILHOUETTE BOOKS IN 1999. SEND US 3 PROOFS OF PURCHASE AND
WE WILL SEND YOU 2 COUPON BOOKLETS WITH A TOTAL SAVING OF
$20.00. (ALLOW 4-6 WEEKS DELIVERY) OFFER EXPIRES
DECEMBER 31, 1998.

••

I accept your offer! Please send me a coupon booklet(s), to:

NAME: _____

ADDRESS: _____

CITY: _____ STATE/PROV.: _____ POSTAL/ZIP CODE: _____

Send your name and address, along with your cash register
receipts for proofs of purchase, to:

In the U.S.	In Canada
Harlequin Books	Harlequin Books
P.O. Box 9057	P.O. Box 622
Buffalo, NY	Fort Erie, Ontario
14269	L2A 5X3

PHQ4982

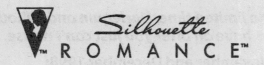

Silhouette
™ R O M A N C E ™

COMING NEXT MONTH